LAWRENCE SCOTT is from Trinidad and Tobago. His first novel, *Witchbroom*, was shortlisted for the 1993 Commonwealth Writers Prize: Best First Book in the Caribbean and Canada. *Witchbroom* was also a BBC *Book at Bedtime* in 1993, for which it received considerable critical acclaim. He was a guest author at the Harbourfront International Festival of Authors, Toronto in 1993.

His short stories have been published in journals and anthologies internationally, and a number of them have been read on BBC Radio 4. He was the winner of the 1986 Tom-Gallon Award for the short story 'The House of Funerals', which is included in this collection. He teaches English at The Sixth Form Centre, City and Islington College, London. ✷

To the Havelaars Snr,

with our love.

Robin & Jeannie.

✷ This is my colleague at work — an English teacher who writes fiction!

LAWRENCE SCOTT

BALLAD FOR THE NEW WORLD

And Other Stories

Heinemann

Heinemann Educational Publishers
A Division of Heinemann Publishers (Oxford) Ltd
Halley Court, Jordan Hill, Oxford OX2 8EJ

Heinemann: A Division of Reed Publishing (USA) Inc.
361 Hanover Street, Portsmouth, NH 03801-3912, USA

Heinemann Educational Books (Nigeria) Ltd
PMB 5205, Ibadan
Heinemann Educational Boleswa
PO Box 10103, Village Post Office, Gaborone, Botswana

FLORENCE   PRAGUE   PARIS   MADRID
ATHENS   MELBOURNE   JOHANNESBURG
AUCKLAND   SINGAPORE   TOKYO
CHICAGO   SAO PAULO

First published by Heinemann Educational Publishers in 1994

Series Editor: Adewale Maja-Pearce

British Library Cataloguing in Publication Data
A catalogue record for this book is available from the British Library.

Cover design by Touchpaper
Cover illustration by John Brennan
Author photograph by Richard Whitehead

ISBN 0435 98939 1

Phototypeset by Wilmaset Ltd, Birkenhead, Wirral
Printed and bound in Great Britain
by Cox & Wyman Ltd, Reading, Berkshire

94 95 96 97 10 9 8 7 6 5 4 3 2

CONTENTS

Acknowledgements

Some of these stories have been published previously, sometimes in slightly different forms, in: *Trinidad & Tobago Review, 1984, 1985*; *Chelsea 46* (New York, 1987); *PEN, 1988*; *Winters Tales* (Constable, 1988, 1989); *Colours of a New Day* (Lawrence & Wishart–Penguin, 1990); *Caribbean New Wave* (Heinemann, 1990); *Pen International, 1990, 1993*; *Telling Stories: The Best of BBC Radio's Recent Fiction* (Coronet–Hodder & Stoughton, 1993).

I would like to thank Marjorie Thorpe, Ken Ramchand, Peter Day, Robin Baird-Smith, Stephen Hayward, Sarah Lefanu, Stewart Brown, Duncan Minshull and my present editor Ruth Hamilton-Jones for their critical and creative insight. Thanks are also due to the many friends who have encouraged and offered suggestions along the way, or just read. I am particularly grateful to Caroline Griffin, Julian Zinovieff, Maggie Wilkinson, Astra, Margaret Busby and above all Jenny Green for close critical and editorial suggestions. I would like to thank, too, Elizabeth Fairbairn, my agent, for warm discretion and sound judgement.

For Earl, Ken, Jenny and Nicky
and
in memory of my mother, Hélène Marie Schoener Scott née Lange
(1901–1993)

'I'm in that huge old house . . . that sense of night-time foreboding which dominated my whole childhood still persists.'

Gabriel Garcia Marquez, *The Fragrance of Guava*.

'It's strange growing up in a very beautiful place and seeing that it is beautiful. It was alive. I was sure of it. There was something austere, sad, lost, all these things.'

Jean Rhys, *Smile Please*.

Malgrétoute

'Boy, when cocoa was king.' That's what they used to say. Then the estate had begun to die. In his textbook on tropical agriculture, *Diseases of Crop-Plants in the Lesser Antilles* by W. Nowell, Mr Wainwright remembered the description. It was a fungus which had come on the winds from Suriname on the South American mainland.

'Look, boss,' Bosoon, the groom, pointed out the young cocoa tree near the verandah of the house at La Mariana. 'Look, in the fork of the branch.' It was a bruise on the bark of the tree. By the next day several shoots had appeared and by the end of the week they were a mass of interlacing twigs. Witchbroom. Then the leaves of the young tree had died after becoming soft and flimsy and the other shoots were grossly deformed. 'Boy, when cocoa was king.'

'When cocoa was king?' He could hardly remember. The damp morning air made him brace himself and rub his forearms vigorously; rub some warmth into the bones which were already arthritic in the elbows. Forty was not too old, he thought, made him think of death, though. He could start over again. Malgrétoute. This was where they had dumped him. Look at it, he thought. Each morning it was there as he stood at the top of the steps on the gallery, looking out over the sugar-cane estate on the edge of the gulf down by Mosquito Creek into which the stinking Cipero River seeped, clogged with the refuse from the black galvanised barrack-rooms huddled in the gully encircling the junior overseer's house. A junior overseer, this was what he had become. He surveyed the scene like this each morning, each and every morning since he had arrived at Malgrétoute, in this fraction of the dawn, this half an hour which was his before his wife and children got up and before the servants began to pester his wife.

1

This was it, a junior overseer on a run-down sugar-cane estate. 'Boy, when cocoa was king.'

He pushed open the Demerara window by the kitchen sink, filled the kettle with water and lit the wick of the kerosene stove. He couldn't die now. No. He couldn't die now. He didn't believe that. There was more, much more ahead, he thought, in spite of all that had happened, there must be more ahead. And then he thought of the sleeping children, six of them and his wife. No. He didn't want them getting up now. This was his time, his half an hour. The flame went out and he had to light the wick again. The black sooty smoke curled off the dirty wick and caught the back of his throat. While the kettle began to boil he went down the rickety back stairs across the back yard to the latrine under the kimeet tree. As he approached the hut he inhaled the heady, strong perfume which came from the white wild lilies which liked to grow in the moist seepage behind the latrine. As he peed he wondered at this apparent contradiction in nature, how the wild lilies with their satiny petals opening out of shiny green stems, already beginning to unfurl to the first light and warmth, amidst the thick fleshy leaves, and reveal their golden centres with their dusty stamens of pollen, had chosen the nastiest place to grow and startle the world. As he buttoned up his crotch he wondered at that. No, he wouldn't die. 'Bosoon, Bosoon, is that you?'

'Yes, boss.'

'It's cold, boy.'

'Yes, boss, it cold no arse. Excuse, excuse, boss. It cold like hell.'

'No, Bosoon. You're right, it cold no tail. It damp.' He could talk to Bosoon. The groom came out from under the house muffled up against the damp. Bosoon had come with him from La Mariana. He knew that Bosoon would stand by him. The black man would stand by him. He knew that.

Bosoon had grown up at La Mariana and picked cocoa for his father as a boy. Bosoon was his groom and now at Malgrétoute he was the watchman too, and then he didn't have anywhere to live, so he lived under the house. Bosoon would always be there. He didn't like his wife calling Bosoon to take messages in the shop. Bosoon was his man.

'Things still bad, eh boss?'

'Yes, Bosoon, things still bad.'

2

'I don't understand this thing, boss, no promotion except into dead man's boots. That is what he does say. The big manager man, how he not call you yet? Them is English people, boss, they don't understand. This thing gone back a long way. Gone back a long way yes. You and me, me and you, me and your father. That is a long time, yes boss. You going to have to kill somebody.'

'Here, Bosoon, drink it while it's hot and strong.' Mr Wainwright laughed. Bosoon lit a cigarette and stood outside at the top of the back steps. Mr Wainwright stood in the doorway and the two men were wrapped in the smoke and the steam and the aroma of the tea. 'Yes, Bosoon, it's a long time.'

'I go stay, boss. I not moving unless you move.'

When he put the cup of tea on the bedside table, moving the rosary beads with his fingers as he placed the cup and saucer down, Mr Wainwright decided again that he would go and see Robertson the G.M. He would go to the General Office and he would get Bosoon to ride with him. Bosoon liked to ride. He could ride Hope while Mr Wainwright rode Prudence. 'Tea, dear.' He looked at his wife and saw six children and he couldn't really remember how it had come to this or for that matter how it had been. He didn't like to think now about how it had been. He still had a picture of her in his Bible when she was sixteen, long before he knew her. He looked at her now and saw his six children. It made him feel guilty that he didn't feel like that now as he had then. They didn't really talk, but they had an understanding. She was feeling it too as she still sat under the mosquito net, dangling her feet on to the damp pitchpine floor, feeling it every single day. She was feeling it too, the change, the disappointment; a disappointment for him though not in him. At least he didn't think it was in him, though at times he wondered, like last night when her brothers came out for a drink and everyone had drunk a lot of rum.

'You are the junior overseer on a run-down sugar-cane estate. What are we now?' She had got confidence from her brothers to say that and they too were sticking in their oars.

'Come on man, get into business man, agriculture is a dead end and cocoa dead, boy.'

'When cocoa was king,' the other brother laughed as he took another swig of rum. 'When cocoa was king.'

'Now is the motor-car, boy. No cocoa, no sugar. What you want to stay in this dump for and work for a set of limey people?'

He looked at his wife and saw six children.

'You can sell any blasted thing to the Americans on the base, and there is oil man, the new El Dorado. You didn't know that is what they come here for originally, gold. Well, that is the new gold, El Dorado, oil.'

He wasn't going to sell any blasted motor-cars and he wasn't going to be a salesman. He was a planter. His overseers knew him as a planter. They knew what he stood for. He stood for fairness, or for a kind of justice, an old justice when everything had its place. He worked hard and his men worked hard. They knew where they stood and he knew what he was, a manager, a planter on his father's cocoa estate. No, he wasn't going to go the way of his wife's brothers, become a businessman and live in a house in town. He wasn't going to leave the land and he wasn't going to stop managing and growing on this land. Bosoon, that was all he had left now, Bosoon. Bosoon would stay by him. Yes, he would take Bosoon this afternoon and go to Robertson. He could hear Robertson as he had heard him before. 'No promotion, except into the boots of a dead man.' Well he wasn't going to die and he wasn't going to wait for anyone else to die. He felt a new confidence as he walked across the drawing-room and began opening up the house. There was just the slightest discernible limp as he crossed the room with the heavy mahogany furniture standing all around him. The children from the barracks used to call him cork foot. He had had polio as a child. He opened up the Demerara windows and let the light, now that the dawn was over, lift the pall off the couch, the sideboard, the oval table with the six chairs, the cabinet and the trolley. They too had come with Bosoon from another place, from La Mariana.

He nearly cut himself shaving. He stirred some more lather into the wooden shaving-bowl and brushed it into his growth. He was afraid of these new hopes. There had been mornings like this before when he had noticed the lilies and gained hope and had had a good smoke with Bosoon and talked of old times. This had lifted him up, especially when Bosoon had made his promise, as he had done many times before, that he would stay and that he would not leave him. There had been times like this before. He could hear his wife fussing

4

over the children and shooing the flies off the food on the breakfast table. Flies. Dysentery. 'Sybil, cover the food, girl.' The mesh of the window screens was ripped and the flies came in hordes and alighted on the food and the baby's bottles and the little boy was down with dysentery. That was all there, just the other side of the door. He could hear his wife pestering the cook that the maid had been late again. He was getting to look old, he thought, as he saw his masked face in the mirror. No, he was the same. There was a way in which you didn't notice how you were changing and then all of a sudden you could see it. An older man. Well there could be dignity in that. He had seen his father grow with dignity, tall, silver-haired and a planter gone before him. He wasn't going to sell any blasted motor-cars. A thought crossed his mind that his sons would leave the land. Maybe it would be oil for them, maybe he was the last. 'No promotion except into dead men's boots.'

When it was after lunch and Sybil was brushing the crumbs off the dining-room table and a silence which was the silence of midday heat and the only sounds were the creaks of the wooden house, Bosoon came up the gravel road from the estate yard with two horses and tethered them under the mango tree at the front of the house.

'I leave it in God's hands,' Mr Wainwright's wife said to herself or her husband as she lay next to him on the big brass bed, resting. 'I leave it in God's hands.' The perfume of the wild lilies rose with the heat from the yard below the bedroom window. 'I must pick some lilies for Father Sebastian and ask him to get Mrs Goveia to put them on Our Lady's altar.'

This was one of the first thoughts which Mr Wainwright had as he and Bosoon rode out of the yard on their way to the general manager's office, imagining his wife with the wild lilies in her arms going into the town to see Father Sebastian. She had her priests. Something was on her mind. He had seen in her eyes the signs of a pilgrimage as she left the house; someone with a purpose to her visit and the lilies were an offering. She was lucky the way she could assail the gates of heaven. She made him feel it was a kind of battle. He remembered standing once outside the bedroom door when she and the children were saying the family rosary and he remembered the prayer which he heard his wife reciting, 'armies set in battle array'. For him the lilies were wild and belonged in the dawn where he could

5

see them when he went to pee. For his wife they were an offering to supplicate and adorn the Virgin Mary's altar for some intention. She had her own intentions this afternoon.

They had their different journeys, he thought. Once, too, she was wild and black-haired with deep brown eyes. Once, too, she had been wild.

The two men didn't talk and Bosoon rode just behind on Hope; Mr Wainwright was on his favourite horse, Prudence.

'Wainwright.' He had been asked to wait on the gallery outside the G.M.'s office overlooking the factory. Then he was called. Robertson was a fat man in a brown suit with a collar and tie which didn't suit the climate and he was red-faced and sweaty. His white skin puckered in the folds of flesh around the collar. 'Good to see you, my good man. Come in and have a seat.' He indicated the leather upholstered chair in front of the general manager's desk. Above, the ceiling fan whirled and hummed making the papers flutter on the desk. 'Well, what can I do for you? You've come all this way from Malgrétoute. What can I do?'

It always took Mr Wainwright a while to believe that this was true: that these words were in fact what the G.M. actually meant, because they were exactly the same each time, pretending in their insinuation that he, Mr Wainwright, had never been here before and that Robertson himself was a complete innocent, there, for him, had given up his afternoon entirely to listen to him as if he had never listened to him before, hadn't an inkling what it was Mr Wainwright had ridden all the way from Malgrétoute for. At first he did not know what to say, how to speak the truth in the face of someone who was lying. Wainwright knew that Robertson was a liar. He waited for him to stop lying, which eventually he did, reluctantly.

'Well, Wainwright, you know it has nothing to do with me. You know that don't you?'

Mr Wainwright didn't reply. He stared at Robertson. He wasn't going to respond to lies. He wondered whether God, in whose hands this all was, would actually look down, as his wife seemed to indicate, surveying the two men and would somehow inspire Robertson to tell the truth. Maybe the Holy Ghost, to whom his wife was constantly appealing for wisdom, and who could conveniently take the form of a dove, would perhaps fly in through the open window and alight on

6

Robertson's desk. Mr Wainwright smiled ironically. 'I leave it in God's hands.'

'You see, I can see that you know that, old man. It's those people at the head office in the Strand. When the director comes down in the summer I will put it to him.'

'The summer?' Mr Wainwright did not intend to speak. 'You mean August holidays?' It was a small assertion but Robertson took the point reluctantly as he wiped his brow and then blew his nose into the same handkerchief. Mr Wainwright was intolerant of people who didn't take care of personal hygiene. He himself looked fresh in front of Robertson in his Aertex shirt and pressed khaki pants. 'We only have two seasons here and this is the dry season, a very dry season.' Mr Wainwright surprised himself. He didn't normally speak metaphorically. Maybe it was a way of avoiding, for the moment anyway, the direct confrontation which would eventually have to take place and it surprised him how Robertson could appear to forget the previous confrontations, but then he had not taken them far enough.

'Well, you know what I always say . . .'

'No promotion except into a dead man's boots,' Mr Wainwright quickly filled in.

'Quite,' said Robertson.

'Well, who are you going to kill?' asked Mr Wainwright.

'What?'

'Who are you going to kill?' Mr Wainwright could hear Bosoon that morning. He could still taste the tea and smell the wild lilies. He knew that Bosoon would be just outside sitting at the bottom of the concrete steps. Uncharacteristically Mr Wainwright started to laugh out loud over and over again. 'No promotion except into a dead man's boots. Well, you're going to have to kill somebody, that is what I'm telling you and if you don't kill somebody, well, you never know what might happen.' He began to laugh again, got up and walked around Robertson's office. He didn't take any notice of Robertson. He opened the office door and shouted, 'Bosoon'.

'Now, Wainwright, nothing stupid.' Bosoon ran up the stairs and was at the door in a minute.

'Yes, boss?'

'The horses. I've just told Mr Robertson that he will have to kill somebody. He will have to find me a pair of boots.'

'Yes, boss.'

'Wainwright.'

'Next time you call me, Robertson, I want to hear that you have a pair of boots for me and I don't want to know who the dead man is.'

In the yard at Malgrétoute Bosoon said, 'You get him, boss, you get him. He didn't know what hit him. Is what I told you this morning. He going to have to kill somebody.'

That evening Mr Wainwright noticed that his wife didn't speak and she didn't ask how he had got on. He felt that he couldn't really tell her what he had said. It now seemed too extravagant and quite crazy and out of character what he had said to Robertson. What had got into him?

The next morning, early, when he was still enjoying the smell of the lilies and Bosoon and himself were having their cup of tea on the back steps, the telephone rang and his wife answered it. It was Robertson. He said, 'Wainwright, I've got you a pair of boots.' Mr Wainwright put down the receiver and looked at his wife. She started to cry and he said, 'Don't worry, it's the Holy Ghost.'

'No,' she said, laughing behind her tears. 'It's us, we're going to have another child.'

King Sailor One J'Ouvert* Morning

> *'It's a feeling which comes from deep within,*
> *A tale of joy or one of suffering,*
> *It's editorial in song of the life we undergo,*
> *That and only that I know is true calypso.'*

MIGHTY DUKE

'Come down J'Ouvert morning, find yourself in a band', the first line of the long-time calypso was an insistently repeated refrain: at first hummed; humming breaking into simulated pan; 'ping pong, ping pong', hummed again; 'ping a ling, ping a ling ping pong, ping a ling, ping a ling ping pang, pang pang', hummed by Philip Monagas with pressed lips as he felt the spirit rising inside of himself this carnival Sunday morning as he stepped out on to the cool terrazzo floor on the verandah of the modern concrete apartment up in the Cascade Hills overlooking Port-of-Spain.

'Come down J'Ouvert morning, find yourself in a band', Philip whistled. He could whistle the tune too but he could not remember the rest of the words and no one else seemed to sing them either, this long-time calypso. Just the one line and then the humming which accompanied the way he found himself walking and moving these days, easy and fluid, and then almost on tiptoe wanting to spring into the air. 'Come down J'Ouvert morning, ping a ling ping p'ding.' It was a kind of invocation, a prayer repeated many times like a mantra

---

*Patois abbreviation of *jour ouvert*.

9

which induced and welcomed the madness of the masquerade, Carnival.

Since returning to the island Philip Monagas had been looking forward to the carnival.

He wasn't a tourist and he didn't want anyone taking him for a tourist. He was from here and he wanted to be seen and known for that. It would have to emanate from him, himself inhabit a costume which would come alive when he moved. He saw wings, the wings of the red devil and the butterfly Papillon, Moco Jumbie reaching for the sky on his long stilt legs. He would have to come out and be, be from here. He didn't want anyone to say that he was moving like a tourist, and yet, he didn't want anyone to suspect that he was forcing it, trying to be a local and being anyone but himself.

Like this morning self outside Mr Elcock's parlour when he went to buy the *Express*: 'Honky'. He didn't acknowledge it. His eyes slit and he kept looking straight ahead into the parlour at the pile of *Express* newspapers on the counter. He felt the blood rising into his cheeks. When he turned around he would have to face the fellas. He would have to walk the gauntlet of the fellas on the bridge. 'Honky.'

'Reds.' Did that feel better? A red skin for a white skin? You couldn't belong if you were white. He didn't believe that, and was that the point anyway? Colour. 'Reds.' He felt a tinge of, well at least they think I belong.

He wasn't a red nigger. How did he know that? Did he know that for sure? He was made to understand that through the elaborate mythology of story; those teatime stories told with guava jam, cheese and Crix biscuits. Uncle Andresito had spent months down in vaults of the Cathedral of the Immaculate Conception sorting through the dusty archives until he found the marriage certificate of the first Monagas with the official stamp PERSONAS BLANCAS. Why was Uncle Andresito so concerned? But, what about the other story that his great-grandfather had confessed to the parish priest that they were negro after all? When a particular member of the family turned out dark: 'That is a throwback, child,' they would laugh and say, 'He turn out bad, eh boy!' They would laugh, their peals of laughter ringing round the verandah. They said, too, that it was the Corsican blood. If there was a little crinkly hair they said it was the Spanish blood. Anything but. The insistence. The obsession. And now, here,

10

this morning, on the bridge in Cascade, big carnival Sunday two hundred years later, clutching his *Express* newspaper, Philip Monagas, great-grandnephew of Philippe Monagas who could only write sad stories, burnt with an anger raging in himself with himself in the burning sun. Two hundred years since they come and no racial mix. He didn't believe that. The whole Diego Martin valley populated with black Monagas. Oh, but that is slave masters giving their names to slaves, and yes, Uncle Bertrand had a little thing on the side up on the cocoa estate, but still we pure. Pure white.

'Reds, you ain't look at me yet man.'

Philip turned. 'Yes, yes man, how you doing? I go see you.' He wanted to say, 'Man I isn't an American, you know,' but with a wave of the hand Philip plucked out of his head his carnival mantra, 'Come down J'Ouvert morning, find yourself in a band,' and bounced up the hill wondering what he looked like to the fellas on the bridge, but feeling better in himself for the picong.

This year he would play J'Ouvert. He would play a J'Ouvert mas.

Early morning still. The pan in the valley had started up: ping pong, ping pong. Coming up the valley with the shacks. The sound was iron, iron on iron. Now was not the time for the fine tenor pan like clear crystal drops in Cascade's waterfall Cazabon had painted up the valley. It was a deeper sound, a sound from the belly and the groin calling the people to a meeting with iron beating on iron:

> *Mooma, mooma your son in the grave already*
> *Your son in the grave already*
> *Take a towel and band your belly*

another song, another tune, reaching up from the soul of a village, Calinda's festival, the stick fight in the gayelle, the circle under the rumshop. 'Mooma, mooma, your son in the grave already, your son in the grave already, take a towel and band your belly.' Philip hummed the tune.

Philip didn't know where these feelings came from, making his heart want to burst. He wasn't brought up to have these kinds of feelings. He was brought up to distrust those drums, any drums, the steel band when he was a child, but the excitement and wonder got into his blood in spite of it all, 'That noise'. But then, later, 'Oh, our people are really clever. We have real talent in this island, you know,' when they started to play classical music, and they themselves didn't even play classical music or read books in their house either. Then too, Tassa: 'Josephine, shut those windows the heat will be unbearable, but that noise. Those people will drive me mad with their drumming.' Tassa, coolie drums, coolie music. All Sunday after mass Indian wedding in the afternoon. All night drumming down in the barracks. Tassa, coolie drums, waking terrified. All night, Tassa. 'Can't those people stop that dreadful noise?'

The noise of enslavement and indentureship.

Yes, this year he would play J'Ouvert. He would play King Sailor. Weeks now it was in his mind to play this mas. 'Come on Philip man, come down J'Ouvert morning and find us man.' These were his pardners from up Petit Valley and Maraval, not real friends but fellas and young girls who would greet him as if they knew him from long ago before he went away, school pardners, who wanted him to belong, yes, to belong because they too strove to belong, and by having him in their group would extend them and their sense of belonging.

He wouldn't play pretty mas in one of the big bands Monday and Tuesday during the day. He would play J'Ouvert and then he would lime. Why King Sailor? He had, is truth, a deep urge to play a real dirty mas, to daub himself, his white skin in the blackest coal and shoe polish (you can't get molasses these days) with streaks of blue rinse powder for his face to become a mask and his whole body to transform itself with a fork in his hand, a tail in his arse and an iron chain dragging behind. 'Jab jab. Pay de devil jab jab.' This spectre from his childhood loomed up in his mind to terrify and to excite. Jab Molassi.

'You don't think I should play Jab jab, boy?' Philip asked his friends.

'No man, Jab jab too dirty, play a King Sailor. It go suit you.' But then they too played in mud bands with brown clay and leaves to cover their naked white bodies. 'Yes man, that is the thing, King Sailor will be the thing exactly for you.'

This same Sunday morning as he stood barefoot on the cool terrazzo floor of the verandah, rocking to the persistent iron on iron of the pan in the valley, he remembered what it was like to be small again and waiting with excitement and fear for the first Jab jabs to come up from the barracks and villages on the sugar-cane estate where he grew up. He was swinging from the verandah ledge with his bare feet hardly touching the cool concrete, squeezing his pennies to throw for the Jab jab. He shook his legs with excitement as they came up the gap, beating their iron chains and brandishing their forks. 'Pay de devil jab jab,' beating the rusty bread tin. He threw the pennies into the yard at their feet and they scrambled them up while still continuing their threats, 'Pay de devil jab jab, pay de devil jab jab.' And Josephine hugged him up and together they laughed and cried for them to come back.

There had been envy then too to belong with those little boys; to be one of those who could throw terror into the neighbourhood, but also bring laughter and madness to the day. In the weeks leading up to carnival he had been taken along to the children's carnival shows, dressed up by his mother to try to win the prize at the company club. They would do the circuit: Red Cross, Guaracara Park, Queens Park Savannah and maybe even the Country Club. One year he had been dressed up as a Usine St Madeleine milk bottle with Bristol board, cellophane and a little silver cap, another time as one of the Pope's Swiss Guards and then once on a float as Peter Pan in Kensington Gardens. But what he wanted to be was a Jab jab and to be with those boys from the barracks down the gap out into the estate with bare bodies in the baking sun terrorising the world or at least the estate.

He would play King Sailor. He had improvised some tufts of coloured ribbon as pompoms for his shoes and streamers for his sailor cap and more streamers for the white stick he would use for the special dance, the King Sailor dance. He could see himself chipping down, shuffling and spinning round the white stick, making his entrance into town for J'Ouvert. 'Come down, J'Ouvert morning, find yourself in a band.' Yes, he was feeling good.

He pressed out the white cotton sailor shirt and hung it on a wire hanger behind the bedroom door. Then he pressed the old pair of white sailor pants with the bell bottoms. He sewed the pompoms on to the front of his washy congs. He put them at the foot of the bed and laid out the bell-bottom sailor pants on the bed with the legs flapping over the side and just touching the edge of the washy congs with the pompoms made from ribbons. He was ready, almost. Then he pinned the ribbons into his white stick, trying out the dance, shuffling around and then leant it up in the corner behind the door. He could do the dance. He was ready. Only thing was the sailor cap which sat on the bed all piquéd up with a pink pompom on top looking like a birthday cake. He was ready for town. 'I coming down, I coming down.' These were the songs of bravery when he was alone. He was nervous as hell.

Four o'clock Monday morning. That was the magic hour. It felt like going to bed and getting up for midnight mass. It had that feeling like going to church. And instead of the litany: Tower of Ivory, House of Gold, Ark of the Covenant pray for us, it was his carnival mantra, 'Come down J'Ouvert morning, find yourself in a band.' Jam Jam Jam.

He shut the door behind him easy and went out into the four o'clock darkness resplendently white with ribbons and pompoms: King Sailor, with only the amber streetlight for a moon. He was walking down into town from up in the Cascade Hills. Dogs barking. Cock was crowing since midnight so that was nothing special. Shuffling feet. He could hear the slap of washy cong on the pitch. People coming down. Massing. More people by the savannah. This was more people than midnight mass Christmas-time even with the parang mass they have now. This was more people than Easter vigil, even if they giving new fire and water.

Already he thought that everyone was watching him. And then it was easy because he was watching everybody. People coming out, showing themselves. There was no distinction now. Some people might think that he was a tourist, but they have plenty black tourists too from Brooklyn and Queens, he thought.

People were looking good. Even those who were not playing mas and just had on jeans and T-shirt looked special. This was it. He had been told about it and he had read about it: Carne Vale, Canboulay, Emancipation. J'Ouvert was all these and he was here in the long line and belonging to it. The little steel bands were coming down from the

14

hills behind Port-of-Spain and there was the sound ahead; a sound which was the massing of people and the scraping of pans on the ground, the hooking-up of pans on their sheds and then the final tuning and the fringes on the pan sheds fluttered in the dawn breeze and glittered. A strange quiet. He saw a bat and a skeleton float by. And then it was sudden, in absolute unison, pan pan pan, jam jam jam, as Invaders began to move down Tragarete Road.

Philip couldn't see anybody he knew. Yes, he knew that fella and he waved and said, 'How you going?' to this one and that one there who he now noticed. But they were not the people he had arranged to meet. This was not the band he was supposed to play in. He wanted to step out to look for the people he was supposed to be with, but he couldn't. A stronger force pulled him back, carried him along. When he looked up he could see the tops of the pan sheds like giant hosays rocking and the crowd pressing round. This was J'Ouvert. He didn't have place to do his sailor dance. He expected to have space and then he would be able to do the special dance. He could do the dance. Give him the space he could do the dance.

Then all of a sudden he was pressed right up against the big bass pan and the fella in charge of the section shouted, 'Come man, push. We need you to push.' Philip didn't think that he could have been referring to him so he hesitated and the fella came alongside him and began to push where he was standing and said, putting his arm round Philip's shoulder, 'So pardner, so, push.' Philip began to push. He dropped his King Sailor stick right there in the gutter. He felt a little sorry for that but it did not last long as he continued to push. Then he saw the excitement on the faces of the children who were hanging from bars inside the sheds above the pan players, taking a ride. He was inside and the music was inside him. He was pushing the pan down into town.

'Monagas!' He saw a fella from the band he was supposed to be in. It flashed through his mind where he was supposed to be. Then he was gone.

By Green Corner he got squeezed up on to the pavement. He grabbed

15

a Carib beer from a fella just managing to prize the money out of his sailor pants pocket, and then he was gone, taken along pressed up against people and the sweat of this whole town, chipping down, ping p'ding, jumping up all the way down into Port-of-Spain.

Philip saw the sun rise over Laventille as he stood up in Nelson Street. He stayed with the pan for the whole J'Ouvert on a journey during which he saw the mamaguy and pappyshow of a people playing a mass of defiance and mockery, irony and disguise, in which they enacted their own terrible enslavement and indentureship, transforming it and offering it now as a gift of celebration for all.

He was heady with the excitement, the ritual and the fact of his belonging. The vision he had had of himself resplendently white in pompoms and ribbons with his stick and his fine stick dance was not what he saw at all. He had to laugh for truth as he looked at his King Sailor shirt tied round his neck and his bell-bottom pants rolled up to his knees. He laughed and said to himself as he pushed the pan right back into the pan yard, 'Like I play Jab jab after all.'

The Fitful Muse

'History is fiction, subject to a fitful muse, memory.'

DEREK WALCOTT

I had forgotten the road and depended almost entirely upon her judgement.

'Yes, that's to Mamoral, to the left is Todd's settlement.'

'Are you sure?'

'I know it like the palm of my hand.' She stretched out her palm and I saw there the fine mesh of interweaving paths which were cut into her skin. 'You've forgotten that these are the roads of my girlhood,' she said.

I looked quickly at her, but had to keep my hands on the steering wheel, and eyes on the road.

When we left the Southern Main Road there had been a fine drizzle and now the narrow ribbon of pitch glittered and steamed. I took it gently through the canefields, anticipating her directions to left or right, so that we could begin the climb into the cocoa hills.

I tried to imagine her as a young girl. Of course I had not known her then, but in the end, after much persuasion, she had given me the photograph taken when she was sixteen, which I have always kept and will always keep for ever, as it was kept by him, my father, in his Bible.

She is standing at a carved pedestal which supports a lectern, upon which there is an open book. We had laughed about that. She could not remember the book, and certainly had not been reading it. 'Maybe it wasn't a real book,' she had said and laughed. She is

17

looking straight into the camera. Her face is smooth. I have tried to touch it, but come up against the glass and passage of years. It is an older face now.

'We didn't always have a car,' she said, 'when we were children or when I came with your father.' Her present voice broke into my imaginings. Her voice and my thoughts became one as we went along and she described and remembered. I saw the places that she talked about. I saw the river with the swirling and swishing water at the ford around the feet of the horses, and then came the buggy and we were through. There was the house, La Mariana: a white wooden house, an open verandah, fret-work eaves and panels through which yellow lamplight shone at lampfall like a lantern. I saw through her voice the sloping lawns and the jacaranda tree.

The memory tantalised me, her history rebuked me. 'It's gone now,' I said.

'What, dear?'

She hadn't heard.

'We used to come up from town on the train to Jerningham Junction and then on to Flanagin Town.' I nodded. 'Take the right here to Brasso Piedra,' she said decisively.

We dipped into a gully and then immediately began to climb again into the foothills of Tamana. I felt that the villages had not changed much since she had known them as we moved up from the towns and the plain. The road was narrower; red earth beneath the verges crumbling into gurgling drains clogged with the tania and their broad leaves.

'Stop!' She had recognised the entrance to the gap. 'This is La Mariana.' This was La Mariana, I thought, as I got out of the car and opened the door on her side. The afternoon was torrid. It hummed and buzzed. My skin was moist, hers was sallow.

'I should've brought a cutlass,' I said, as we both looked at the side of the road she insisted was the entrance to the gap. Bits of broken masonry did suggest the ruins of a culvert and a bridge across the drain. 'I should've brought a cutlass,' I said again.

On either side of the road the cocoa trees crowded in, green and purple. Away from the road, away from the sunlight I could see the yellow, green and purple pods. The undergrowth was a tangle of

18

bush and lying close to the ground the wild pink mimosa, Ti Marie, closing her fringes at our touch, keeping us at bay with her thorns.

'I can see Nurse with the three children. She would take them as far as the bridge at the bend in the road.' I followed her stare and the direction of her outstretched arm. I too saw Nurse in her starched white apron buttoned over her fully gathered skirt and her black ironed hair covered with the white starched piqued cap. 'The children,' she said, 'they loved to throw stones into the river.'

I could see the sepia photograph in the old family album.

She was an old woman now remembering her young motherhood and her young children. She had shrunk, standing there on the narrow rutted pitch road with the bush pressing in, pulling its wild self over what had been. She turned to right and left, looking about her, mapping with her outstretched arm the arrangment of her memories: the white wooden house, the sloping lawns, the jacaranda tree, the cocoa house and the barrack-rooms. 'Samuel lived there with Ernestine and their umpteen children. I used to give her my baby clothes when I had finished with them.' Everything was still there as vivid as it had been sixty years before, when she had first come as a young bride to La Mariana on her honeymoon.

We craned our necks above the cocoa on the side of the road to see if we could spot some relic of this past, maybe the high water tank among the cedar trees. 'Next time I will bring a cutlass,' I said, excited by her determination to find the gap, to enter and to find some piece of that past and to stand on it again.

It invited us and rebuked us. The bush, the history it was covering.

'You can turn just beyond the river after the bend in the road,' she remembered. I followed her advice. As we drove away she kept turning around and looking on either side to catch the last glimpses of what was no longer there. She was waving her arms nervously. 'If I could I would come back, buy the land again. Live here till the end.' We smiled and imagined this together.

The way to Tortuga took us through other cocoa estates. 'This was where all the families lived.' We were climbing quite high now with precipices sheer on one side and the forest stacked on the other. In the valleys the cocoa estates. 'This was where everything happened. This was the centre of the world, Gran Gouva,' she demonstrated with a sweep of her arm, 'where the families lived in the great houses. This

19

was where we spent our childhood with our cousins and our uncles and aunts.'

She did know these roads like the palm of her hand. 'I am sure that this is La Vega. Uncle Bernard and Aunt Cecile lived here. She was my father's sister. We called her Sissy, Aunt Sissy. On Sunday mornings we all went to Aunt Sissy's after mass. The church was at the top of Pepper Hill. Mother looked beautiful in an Edwardian gown and Father and the other men set up the targets for shooting, while the servants passed round trays of rum punches. The old aunts spoke French. We sat in the summer house for shade.' She told her story as we drove along.

'Go on,' she said, 'we'll come to San Jose and after that Josefito where Uncle Carl and Aunt Meme lived, and dear Aunt Celeste who managed the estate when her husband died, and she had to bring up nine children alone. They were extraordinary people, she, Celeste.'

'This is Josefito.' At the back of the old house were the outbuildings where the servants and labourers lived, the barrack-rooms. 'They were like the family, our old nannies. They tucked us up in bed. Before that we used to have hot chocolate made from cocoa sticks and warm bakes in the kitchen while the grown-ups were having cocktails. The nannies told us stories about douens and jumbies. Afterwards we had to go along the long corridors with our candles and the huge shadows frightened us. We loved staying with Aunt Sissy.'

All along the road the cocoa trees were in high bush and blight crinkled their branches. 'Malaria was a scourge. Aunty Sissy came to check our nets before she went to bed.'

She urged me on though it was getting late. Through a break in the trees I could see that the sun was going down low over the gulf. 'Go on,' she said. The road was not surfaced. 'I spent a weekend here. I don't remember it being this long. We used to walk to the church at the top of Pepper Hill or sometimes Aunt Celeste would send the groom with the buggy for us.' I had to go slowly because of the road. 'The name will come to me when I see it.' She had become animated as if she was a young girl again and sat up and peered out of the windscreen anticipating at every corner the appearance of the house.

I saw the roof before she did as we came around a bend in the road. It emerged higher than the cocoa trees, but lower than the immortelle. As she saw it she cried, 'Los Naranjos!' We parked under the front verandah. 'It is exactly like it used to be.' It was still in pretty good condition, rising above us on the tall pillar trees. The windows had panels of jalousies on either side and the gables were surmounted with bands of fret-work like lace. We walked round to the back and came into the quadrangle of outhouses and barrack-rooms with a courtyard in the middle. 'I was so happy here,' she said.

'I stayed here once,' I heard my mother tell the young girl who was hanging out the half-door in one of the barrack-rooms. The girl smiled. 'I was a little girl here too, like you.' The girl smiled and turned to her brother who was also swinging on the door. They smiled and I felt embarrassed as my mother told them her life as a young girl. The children stared at us as we gazed at the view and the sloping lawns which fell away from the driveway to the steep bank with the orange trees, from which the estate got its name.

The children's father appeared. 'Good evening.' He nodded. I expected him to say 'Madam', but he didn't.

'I used to stay up here as a child.' He smiled as she spoke.

'Run-down now. You can't get people to work now.'

'The gangs used to work then. Those were happy days.'

I saw the man and his children staring at the car. They left my rear view as I took the bend in the road.

'I was so happy there,' she said again as we made our way back down to the plains through Felicity and Esperance to the new modern highway which cut from north to south through the canefields.

That evening we sat on the porch of the concrete bungalow. 'Turn the porch light off, dear. It will keep the insects away.' The dim light from the drawing-room made us just visible to each other.

I could hear voices in the other houses nearby, dishes being washed and the clatter of knives and forks.

The rest of the world had crowded in.

The tractors had long come in here and bulldozed what had at any rate been barren land and which had lain useless for years.

Fortunes had been invested, won and lost. Cocoa and sugar had died, but the land remained and they put up the pink bungalow with its porch and sold off the rest of the land in lots. Houses sprouted up and the pink bungalow with the porch which the wind used to shake on the open plain was now one of many. Hemmed in. Now she was leaving after more than one hundred years.

The lime trees behind the house were dead. Men from the electricity company had come to cut down the casuarina trees which had died and were entangled in the electricity wires, overgrown with wild vines.

That morning, sitting on the porch, she had pointed to the pink cassia which, they said, looked like cherry blossom. 'Look, do you see the new leaves?' Suddenly they had sprouted, crowding out the last of the pink blossom which had come in the dry season. She had not noticed the blight crinkling the branches. I kept this knowledge to myself, protecting her.

The cassia grew where the poui, planted by my father, had once grown. One morning soon after we had moved him to a nursing home we woke to the fullness of the tree, a full green poui before its yellow glory, flung down, blown down, cracked at the base. The branches pushed against the glass windows of the bungalow. The roots were forced out of the ground. Coming in at the gate that morning Antoinetta the cook had said, 'Like there was a strong wind last night, eh, Madam?' Mr Johnson the overseer, who had stayed on after the close-down of the sugar company, had planted the cassia in memory of my father. The memory was now dying too.

We went to bed early. I woke suddenly to the sound of a nightmare, the voice of a dream. It was my mother in the next room. She was breathing heavily and crying out with a strangulated voice. I went to her. I was naked because of the heat. I pulled out the tucked-in mosquito-net and sat on the edge of the bed next to her and took her hand. She woke startled, crying out and relieved that it was me, and presumably not some phantom of her dream. She turned over. 'I was having a terrible dream. Go off to your bed now, dear.' I sat on the edge of the bed and stroked her hair as she fell back to sleep.

The next morning I asked her to tell me her dream.

She was a little girl dressed in a thin cotton chemise. She was standing outside at the back of one of the large estate houses in the middle of the quadrangle of outhouses and barrack-rooms. She was looking up to the galvanised roofs of the barrack-rooms and rising up out of the barrack-rooms was a huge tall black man dressed in breeches. He was barebacked and his black skin gleamed. He was bearing down on her with a whip.

She said that, when I woke her, she was crying for help.

I never asked her to interpret her dream for me. I thought of the little girl who was happy in Aunt Sissy's garden. I thought of the journey the previous afternoon through the old estates and I thought of the one hundred years of accumulated guilt and fear which had taken hold of her in that dream that night, in the pink bungalow on the plains, near the swamps and the oyster beds, now that she was closing house, leaving the estate.

Rabbits

'I can hardly speak about it,' Marie Wainwright said as she held the earpiece of the telephone firmly in her left hand. She rested her elbow on the sill of the Demerara window and leant towards the phone in order to speak, slightly tipping the tall stool on which she was sitting. Near her arm was a half drunk glass of lemonade, sweating. As she listened to her cousin Inez she stared out into the yard. 'Quite,' she said. Her fingers stroked a few strands of stray hair up the nape of her neck and tucked them into her bun.

The hutches which she could see beneath the pushed-out Demerara shutters of the sugar-cane estate house stood in a line below the kimeet and mango trees. They confronted her with her latest project for saving money: rabbits. They breed so quickly, she thought.

'You had the children with you?' Inez asked.

Marie Wainwright had six children and was at this moment expecting her seventh child. She said she'd gone to Mr Weston's bungalow to ask him to give her and the children a lift into town for the Good Friday service. 'I can hardly talk about it. I've told you everything, I think. Everything, that is, which I dare say.'

She had remembered saying, 'Come back, you'll fall.' Two of her children were running ahead of her. They had looked back and laughed mischievously. 'Come back, you'll smudge your best white pants, your new dress.' She had watched as their shoes, newly polished by Baboolal the yardman, scuffed the larger stones on the gravel road up to Mr Weston's bungalow. She had so wanted to be in time for the reading of the Passion. She'd kept seeing them in front of her and seeing her children standing there before them, staring as children do.

24

'What a trial for you, my dear, what an ordeal.' Inez pulled her back to the telephone conversation.

'I so wanted to be there in time for the Adoration of the Cross and for Communion.' Marie Wainwright spoke distractedly and remembered Mrs Weston's auburn hair in the afternoon sun against her white English skin as she lay with her arms outstretched like a cross on the cushions beneath the tamarind tree.

'Mr Weston?' Inez enquired.

'I called, but the house was empty.' Marie Wainwright looked about her own empty dining-room. Out of the silence came the metal chink of hoes on the gravel outside. A gang of women from the barracks were weeding the yard.

Then they stopped, and she could see them squatting below the mango tree, taking some shade. One of the women was pregnant. She squatted with her big belly, pushing her skirts down between her legs. Marie Wainwright watched the women from the barracks under the mango tree near the rabbit hutches. They breed so quickly, she thought.

'You see, the children had run into the yard ahead of me. They always loved that big yard with the tamarind tree,' she explained to Inez. Tamarinds were in season. 'When I got to the top of the verandah steps the door was open and I called.'

'The children?' Inez asked.

'The children? Their innocence protected them. They don't talk about it, we don't talk about it. When I came downstairs I called for them, but they did not answer, and then I went looking for them.'

'You mustn't talk about it, Marie. Why don't you meet me at the club tonight. It's library night, you remember?'

'Yes, the club, the library, yes. I will have to get the girl to stay with the children.'

'You must prepare yourself,' Inez continued. 'They are talking about it.'

'At the club. How on earth?'

'It seems that after you and the children had left, a couple of young overseers turned up with some of the young girls. You know the type? And now it's all over the company.'

'How dreadful. Poor Mr Weston. I can't help thinking about him. Imagine a mother doing that. The house was so empty and they, they

25

under the tamarind tree, all the cushions.' Marie Wainwright remembered the cushions and Mrs Weston's auburn hair.

As she spoke she picked off beads of condensation from the glass of lemonade and then touched her brow with the tepid moisture.

'Don't, Marie, don't think about it. Put it from your mind. Those are dreadful people, quite different. It would never have happened so in our mothers' day.'

As she stared out of the Demerara window Marie Wainwright could see Baboolal going to clean out the rabbit hutches. The women from the barracks had begun again the rhythmic chink of the hoes on the gravel.

'I will see you at the club at six.'

'Bye.' Marie Wainwright put down the phone.

The house was silent. As she listened it creaked, and she could hear the wind in the palmiste.

'Madam?'

'Josephine, a nice glass of lemonade. This heat is killing me.'

'Yes, madam.'

'Josephine, a dash of bitters.'

'Yes, madam.'

'Those rabbits.' She suddenly remembered. 'Baboolal!' She leant from the window and shouted into the yard, 'Baboolal!' The man rose from where he was stooping. He stopped weeding the orange and red zinnias and looked up at her.

'Madam?'

'Baboolal, the rabbits.' And then she remembered that she had seen him cleaning out the hutches. 'You've fed the rabbits?'

'Yes, madam.'

The garden behind the rabbit hutches was wild with grass the people called rabbit meat. The Wainwright children liked to call it that too, and Marie Wainwright herself referred to the grass as rabbit meat. It was precious and she had to see that Baboolal put a stop to the barrack children with their grass knives.

The barracks huddled there, black galvanised one-room shacks, erected along the grass track beyond the pasture behind the wild garden.

They had started with just two rabbits and now they had quite a number. They bred so quickly.

She made herself comfortable on the couch under the window in the gallery near the pots of angel-hair fern. Her knitting was in a sewing-bag on the floor beside her. Yes, she would take it up in a moment, but she just wanted to close her eyes for a few minutes. She moved and made herself more comfortable, cradling her pregnant stomach in her arms.

She tried to remember what she had seen:

'Come here at once.' She had wanted to put her hands over their eyes. The children were standing in front of the couple, who were lying on the cushions, and staring. It was Mrs Weston's freckled back and her auburn hair in the afternoon sun which had stung her own eyes. She had noticed the pattern on the cushions, thinking that she had seen the very same gold and brown English country flowers and had thought of getting it for the drawing-room couch and chairs. 'Let us find Mr Weston, he must be at the back of the house.' She remembered saying that. The children were rooted and she had found it difficult to turn her eyes away. It seemed like hours, when it must have been only a few seconds, before she dragged the children away, talking to herself and them, and saying 'Excuse me, excuse me,' over and over again. She had wanted to look back in case she had dropped something, all the time keeping the Crucifixion before her eyes.

All she'd kept seeing was the freckled back of Mrs Weston, her pale English skin in the sun, her auburn hair in the afternoon. It was Mr Poole, wasn't it? She remembered his brown hands. She remembered the shoes and socks on the gravel path beneath the tamarind tree. The socks were navy blue and the shoes brown. He had turned his face towards her and the children, but he could have been blind because he looked beyond her and the children, rapt. She remembered now that they had not even moved from that position. She hated to think about it. The woman's freckled back, the naked toes, the shoes and socks. They had not noticed them, she and her two small children, rooted there under the tamarind tree on a Good Friday afternoon. Then she remembered the woman's sandal near her ankle.

She had dragged the children away ignoring their questions. 'What is Mrs Weston doing, Mummy?' She had put her hand over her daughter's mouth. She did not want what she had seen to reach the light of words. She did not want this to be her daughter's realisation.

'Close your eyes.' She could see the Pietà, the Mother of Sorrows with her dying son draped in her arms, her heart pierced with arrows. 'Offer it up,' she had said to herself.

The zinnias in the naked flower beds, after Baboolal had weeded them, looked ragged in the sun. So little grew in the dry season, so little, close to the ground. But the trees flowered, the blood of the flamboyant, the red of flame and blood.

The rabbits were nibbling the fresh rabbit meat oblivious of the woman's presence. In the last hutch, which she inspected, there were two rabbits, one humped upon the other's back. She stared at them and lost herself in the staring. The pregnant woman rocked back on her heels and rubbed her hands into her hips. She was lost here for a moment which seemed like an eternity. The female rabbit continued to nibble and to twitch its nose, its face a continual movement of pink and white. The male stared ahead, and the movement of that passion was imperceptible, then suddenly the slightest trembling of the small body and hardly an audible squeak. As she continued to stare, the heat made her drowsy and she could feel the sun on her bare shoulders. She could see the freckled back of the English woman's white skin, the rapt face of Mr Poole, his brown fingers in her hair.

'Madam, I finish the cleaning out.' Baboolal stood watching his madam looking at the rabbits humped one upon the other. She did not move. 'Madam, I finish.' She turned and looked through him.

Marie Wainwright rested. On the bedside table were the paraphernalia of her religion: rosary beads, a mother-of-pearl crucifix, a bottle of holy water, another bottle shaped in the image of Our Lady of Lourdes and filled with water from that miraculous shrine. Above her bed was a picture of the Sacred Heart, and behind the frame was a dried palm from the Palm Sunday procession. She had pinned a medal of Saint Gerard Majela, the patron saint of safe pregnancies, to the lapel of her housecoat.

She began the rosary, beginning with the Five Sorrowful Mysteries. 'The first mystery is the Agony in the Garden.' She meditated on the Passion. When she closed her eyes she saw the rabbits humped one upon the other. She saw their soft vacant eyes. 'And lead us not into temptation.' She saw the tamarind tree and the cushions heaped beneath it. 'And now and at the hour of our death.' The freckled back, Mrs Weston's white English skin, her auburn hair. 'The fruit of thy womb.' She saw the rapt face of the overseer.

The rosary slipped from her fingers and fell to the pitchpine floor making the sound of beads rattling in a calabash.

As she walked across the golf course and took the path around the tennis courts, she wondered whether Inez would be there, or would she have to speak with the English ladies who sat in groups on the Morris chairs drinking gin. 'My dear Marie, we never see you now.' That would be Blanche Selness whose husband was an engineer and had two blond children. The others would ask about her boys, 'And what are your boys up to now?' And of course she always thought the boys had done something dreadful again.

The younger ones and the more recent arrivals from England would call her Mrs Wainwright. She would smile and walk on. And always there would be the whispers, and once she had overheard one of those whispers: 'Thinks she's a duchess.' Poor people, she thought, so little breeding, a new breed coming out after the War.

This evening they would be talking about the Poole and Weston affair and they would know that she knew and that she had seen Mrs Weston without any clothes on below the tamarind tree with the naked Mr Poole. The young overseers and their young girlfriends would have seen her and her children retreating down the gap on Good Friday afternoon.

The English ladies were lying in easy chairs, sipping gin or rum and soda, which the barman was just then serving on a tray.

Coming in from the darkness she blinked. She had to cross the full width of the ballroom to get to the alcoves where the library books were kept. She hoped that Inez would be there. She could not see her, just the English ladies laughing and sipping.

29

'Oh, Marie.' It was Phyllis Mellors. 'My dear, how marvellous to see you at the club!' Marie Wainwright smiled.

'You must come and sit down with us, Marie.' They pronounced her name as if it were English and not French, so that it sounded like Murray. It wasn't she that they were calling, Marie Wainwright thought, as she retreated from the Morris chairs, seeing Inez out of the corner of her eye.

They would want to talk about Mrs Weston and question her. The baby moved inside her and discreetly she put her hand on her stomach. 'I must just get some books.' This completed her retreat. She addressed this to the group of ladies in the easy chairs, but to no one in particular. When she turned she could feel their eyes. Then she heard the high-pitched English voice, like a dart in her back. They were not whispering. They were giggling, 'Some people are always pregnant, they breed just like rabbits.' Marie Wainwright hurried to the ladies' room. Bending over the white Armitage basin, she vomited, feeling her child heave inside her.

She sat thinking only of her baby, sweating and feeling faint. She took a small bottle of eau-de-Cologne from her handbag and inhaled deeply from the unstoppered bottle.

Outside the window in the darkness she could hear the caddies, the Indian boys from the barracks, laughing. She believed they were laughing at her.

Chameleon

Monty was born in a large old colonial house in the town of Villahermosa near Merida, through which the Magdalena seeped, muddy and clogged with waterlilies. It was a town inhabited by tall men, renowned for its generals and young men who were trained to be generals because their fathers wanted it to be so. Monty's father had wanted to be a general. He admired Sir Winston Churchill in England and he had wanted Monty to be a general one day too.

But he himself never became a general, but continued all his life to dream of becoming one. When Monty was born, at his baptism he was named after General Montgomery – Monty, the desert rat – for which a special dispensation had to be granted by the Pope in Rome through the Apostolic Nuncio in Caracas. His mother would have liked to have christened him Jesus.

The little boy grew, but he was pale.

His legs were thin and cold like a lizard's which made him seek the naked stones in the sun to warm his cold reptilian skin. 'Come, Monty, sit in the sun,' his mother Emelda called. 'Sit by the geraniums.' The boy turned and smiled at his mother as he sat next to the pot of red geraniums.

But when his father saw him he said, 'Straighten your back.' This was something that his father would often say. Monty got up and stood like a little Napoleon with his hands behind his back and looked out over the plain below the walled town of Villahermosa towards the Magdalena whose source was in the Andean foothills. 'Now, walk like a man,' his father said.

In the end his father relented. The thin-legged lizard showed no signs of becoming the kind of boy who would one day be the kind of man who would become a general, though each day his father told him to straighten his back and to walk like a man.

Monty learnt to play the harp at Señor Figuera's, an old man who at the time of the civil war had not wanted to be a soldier or become a general, but preferred to sew and to be a tailor. Playing the harp had been passed down in Señor Figuera's family and he decided to pass it on to Monty because he had never married and had no sons. 'Send him after school,' he told Emelda. 'I will teach him to pluck the harp.' Monty learnt to play the harp well because it was a serious business for Señor Figuera. He also learnt to play the *cuatro* and could play a *joropo* and an *aguanaldo* and he even learnt to play the rumba and samba which came up the rivers on the barges with the travelling black musicians and circus people from Brazil and Colombia.

Monty, with his long fingers for plucking the harp, grew to have long legs; thin long legs which he still used to lay out in the sun on the naked stones near the pots of red geraniums even though he was now sixteen and his father's impatience with his undeveloping physique was now irreversible. Instead, he was turning his attention to his young nephew to see if he would fulfil his dream of becoming a general.

However, it had been some years before this final turning away that there was an occasion of much greater disappointment for Monty's father.

At one end of the patio of the large old colonial house there was a trellis of white lattice-work through whose filigree lacy shadows played on the stone floor. This was particularly true at siesta-time when the house was completely silent and the heat sizzled outside and there was a scherzo of lizards among the dry almond leaves. If you were standing on the verandah, looking out over the plain of Villahermosa, you would not have been able to see the Magdalena because of the blinding glare. The only sound was the cry of the cigale calling for rain, and the lizards, 'In this vale of tears, this *lacrimarum valle*,' as Emelda was accustomed to repeat.

Monty had kept the secret since before his First Communion which took place when he was seven years old and the parish priest Father Rosario thought that he had truly arrived at the age of reason and could distinguish between good and evil.

32

When he was six Emelda allowed him to take his siesta on the patio in the hammock which hung between two banyan trees. He had been afraid of the dark in the shuttered room, and of the web of the mosquito-net. Monty never muttered a word, not even to his nurse Ernestina who together with Emelda looked after the boy and would leave him alone to sleep when she had seen him dozing safely in the hammock. 'Now, sleep my Montyquito,' she whispered as she tiptoed into the house.

When it first happened it seemed like a dream, partly caused by the strange unreality created by the peculiar silence of the siesta-time, the heat which turned the head and the glare which mesmerised the eyes. The day Monty first told me his tale he said that it had been the sound of splashing water which had first alerted him; splashing as it were into the basin of a fountain over and over again with the same force and regularity (like the fountain in the middle of the square at the centre of Villahermosa), but he admitted that these associations must have most certainly been created by the madness of the siesta. I remember now that when he first told me the tale we had been sitting in the botanical gardens and there had indeed been a fountain playing in the dip near the bougainvillaea arbour, and at the time he had pointed to it in recognition. Also, it had been siesta-time, but we were not asleep because it was now a different culture in a different place. This was the island of La Trinidad off the mainland, where the British had ruled for so long bringing their cold habits.

While I wonder about these things now, I didn't at the time.

He was awakened from his six-year-old slumber by the sound of water splashing over and over again, so that hardly had it awakened him, than it seemed to be hushing him back to sleep again. This was how he had begun his story. What seemed to be a kind of regularity stopped and it was this sudden change which eventually startled him and made him sit up in the hammock more alert than usual. He then slipped out of the hammock and stumbled in his cotton chemise towards the sound of splashing water which seemed to be coming from behind the trellis of white lattice-work. He walked over the lacy shadows which fell from the filigree on to the stone floor.

This trellis of white lattice-work was an unusual feature of the old colonial house which had been in the Monagas family since fifty

33

years before Emancipation. It was unusual because it was a break in the quadrangle of the patio and was in effect a window into the patio of the neighbouring old family house.

Monty pulled himself up on to the edge of the geranium pots and tried to peep through the diamond-shaped lattice. His small fingers gripped where the old paint crumbled. Monty held fast and stared at the little girl Bernadetta who was sitting in a metal bathtub and pouring water over her head and over her naked body with a calabash. Then he became embarrassed and got down off his perch and went back to the hammock and tried to keep his eyes shut.

He said that it happened like this for years. It happened every day for six years and then it stopped abruptly on Bernadetta's twelfth birthday. Every day for six years he would pretend to sleep at siesta-time, when Ernestina thought that he was dozing safely in the hammock, but instead he would climb up on to the geranium pots and peep through the lattice-work at Bernadetta.

Bernadetta was no stranger to Monty. Indeed, they had grown up together and had been taken for walks along the walls of the town by their nurses after siesta-time when the sun had gone down. They had played as small children do, innocently. But, now, some new sensation (he called it that when he first told me the story), some new feeling stirred in him because of the clandestine nature of the experience, peeping through the lattice-work, standing on the edge of the geranium pot. Yet, on the other hand, his peeping had been an act of innocence. He felt it to be so at the time and still did now many years later, though he could see the possibility of an alternative interpretation. He was then only six years old, and when it stopped, twelve or fourteen. He could never quite remember how much older he was than Bernadetta. He could have called to her, but he did not and he never told her and kept it a secret always.

At the end of our first meeting Monty insinuated that the naked Bernadetta was only part of the secret and that if he felt eventually he could trust me, he would tell me the rest of the tale. Clearly, there had been the initial curiosity of the small boy in the naked body of the little girl, but in the end it was not the young girl's nakedness which continued to fascinate the young Monty.

As she grew older, Bernadetta, thinking that she was entirely on her own, would spend time dressing slowly after bathing: towelling,

34

powdering and massaging her body with eucalyptus oil. She used to hang her petticoat and dress over a small bush which was in the sun. Monty would lie in the hammock until he heard the splashing of the water stop and then he knew that she would soon begin dressing. He stared in wonder as she slipped on her silk petticoat and pulled on her crinoline which had been lying on the grass ruffled like the petals of a wild white hibiscus. Then she would pull her dress over her head, put her arms into the sleeves and then fluff the skirt out making it stick out like a star. He loved it when she then twirled around and laughed to herself, throwing back her head and looking up into the frangipani tree blossoming over her, golden and white. Monty ducked at this moment, in case, looking up, her eyes might fall on him peeping through the lattice.

This was all there was to it, he insisted. I did not press him any further, but I did not at the time believe him and felt that there was some other dénouement to the tale of the little boy whom they called Lizard and whose father had wanted him to be a general. I believed that with time and trust he would tell me the rest of the story.

This was all there was to it: the meditational trance each siesta as he viewed Bernadetta Montero dress herself after bathing in the silence of the siesta.

We had taken to strolling opposite 'Mille Fleurs', the house of a thousand flowers, where there was an avenue of yellow poui and where the coconut-sellers and oyster-vendors set up their stalls at night under the flickering flambeaux.

It was the day of Bernadetta's twelfth birthday and it was an unusually hot day for Villahermosa, and instead of the bedroom shutters being closed, they had been thrown open in frustration by the would-be sleepers who could not rest because of the interminable heat. Monty could have stayed in his room that day, because originally it had been the closed shutters in the daytime which had made him go on to the patio for the siesta because he was frightened. But the habit was now so well-established that no one thought he should change after all these years because of the heatwave.

So as usual Monty lay in his hammock trying to read Cervantes which his mother thought would be good for him. He lay as usual until he heard the splashing of Bernadetta's bath cease and then he crept as usual to the pot of red geraniums, and because now he was quite tall he didn't have to stand on the edge of the pots, but could look over the trellis quite easily. And today he noticed particularly the shadow of the filigree which played with his own shadow on the terrazzo floor of the patio.

Because it was her birthday, Bernadetta had a new dress, a birthday dress spread out over the hibiscus hedge. It was white broderie anglaise and the hem and edges of the puffed sleeves were trimmed with red ribbon. He longed to reach out and touch it and pass the satin ribbons through his fingers. He remained silent – as silent as at the moment of Consecration during mass – during the towelling and powdering of Bernadetta's body: bit his lip in concentration as she played with the dress pressed against her naked body and twirled, pretending to dance and Monty ducked as she threw her eyes up to the canopy of frangipani as she had done every day since she was a little girl and he had first seen her at that very first siesta when she was six or five, when he was frightened and could not sleep behind the closed shutters in the dark and Ernestina had brought him to the hammock and told him to sleep and he had been awakened by the splashing of water as if it were from a fountain. He turned at the sudden crack behind him which he thought was a locust falling from the roof. At that moment, he told me, he remembered that he could hear the distant cry of the cigale, and he thought how good it was that the rain was coming. His father was standing directly behind him. In his concentration he had not felt the older man's presence. In his meditational trance he had not heard him. The crack was not the crack of a locust falling from the roof, but the crack of his father's boot stepping on to a black beetle and breaking its back.

The man who would himself have liked to have been a general and who had long given up hope that this lizard of a son would ever be a general and had pinned his hopes on his younger nephew because he had no other sons, looked past Monty and stared at Bernadetta dancing under the frangipani bush with her white birthday dress pressed against her naked body. He turned away and went to the edge of the patio and looked out over the plain of Villahermosa and strained his eyes to see the Magdalena, but instead had to shade his eyes from the glare.

That evening, as we came to this point in the story, Monty broke off abruptly and said that he would have to go as he had an urgent

36

appointment with a student to whom he was teaching English and that they were reading *The History of the English Speaking Peoples, Volume 2: The New World*, by Sir Winston Churchill.

Later, as I watched him disappear round the corner of Cipriani Boulevard, I smiled as I mused on his reading and felt the oyster from the oyster cocktail slip down my throat.

It was with a certain urgency that I met Monty the following week having had the chance to speculate on where his story might lead. I tried to push Freud to the back of my mind, indeed, to banish him altogether. I did not feel that the doctor of Vienna had a place in the New World and could explain the psychic mythology of a young boy whose dreams were the screams of conquistadorial genocide and whose demons were the lizards of the Galapagos: whose fantasies were in the romantic adornment of a young girl.

Quite unexpectedly Monty invited me back to his small apartment in the old town behind the walls of Lapeyrouse Cemetery. On the way there we talked about the changing town and how some of the balconies still existed at the front of the old town houses which reminded him of Villahermosa and Cartagena where he had been taken every year by his parents for a holiday.

We sat in a small room off the small verandah which was at the top of the low steps just off the pavement and the green moss-furred drain. The old woman from whom he rented the room kept plants and they grew in cut-down kerosene tins painted red and green and stood on the ledge of the wooden verandah. The plants were mostly anthuriums, seed ferns and asparagus fern which climbed the lattice and fell over the front, tangled where it could get a hold.

The room was bare. In one corner was a harp with a stool next to it and on one wall a fairly large family portrait in sepia of a man and a woman sitting on the low wall of the verandah of an old colonial house. The woman had a baby in her arms and standing in the background was a black servant, the baby's nurse. Monty saw my preoccupation with the portrait and identified the man and woman as his mother and father and the black nurse as Ernestina. The baby was himself.

We sipped rum with cubes of ice and talked. Or rather, Monty talked and I listened. Often he would pick up his *cuatro* and strum a chord.

I had left with the vivid image of his father's boot crushing the back of the black beetle on the patio of the house in Villahermosa overlooking the plain and in the hazy distance the River Magdalena. On the other side of the trellis Bernadetta was putting on her birthday dress trimmed with red ribbon. Monty's father continued to strain his eyes in the glare towards the Magdalena. Then without turning he said, 'Go to the tamarind tree at the back of the house and pick me a switch.' Monty did not look at his father but went down the steps and round the back of the house to the back yard where the tamarind tree grew and in whose branches he had played as a small boy. He broke off a thick switch from one of the lower branches and on his way back to the patio cleaned off the twigs and leaves with his penknife. He signalled to me with two fingers joined together to indicate the thickness of the switch.

He told the story methodically now. There were no embellishments. He did not digress to tell me of the cigale, of the River Magdalena, or of the trellis or how the water falling from Bernadetta's calabash reminded him of the fountain in the middle of Villahermosa. He stood behind his father and waited. He told me that when he recalled this moment, as he had done on many occasions and in many dreams which had found their own metaphors, he remembered that his mind was a black hole of nothing. Again I tried to banish the doctor of Vienna, Thebes, the crossroads, the murder, the plague. This was a new world. Occasionally, he said, there was a ripple of white and red. This tender image was fleeting and did not bring much solace at that precise moment, though it did subsequently. His father then said, 'Take off your trousers and bend over.' He pulled down the boy's pants and whipped him sixteen times and then told him to pull up his pants and trousers and go to his room.

At that point I got up and went out on to the little adjoining verandah with the old lady's anthuriums and seed ferns. I looked out into the silent and empty street. I heard behind me in the room, the harp, plucked twice. I was holding my glass with rum and ice and I brought the glass up to wet my lips, but I did not swallow the alcohol. My throat was tight and I found it difficult to swallow. When I re-entered the room Monty had his back to me: a small back of a slight man caught in the act of plucking the harp for the third time. I sat behind him. He turned and smiled.

He then got up and came towards me and took my hand. 'Come,' he said, 'come and see. I think I want to show you. I think I can show you. I think I can trust you.' He led me into his bedroom, knelt next to an old chest and lifted the lid, resting the back gently against the concrete wall. 'Look,' he said. From the chest he lifted a white broderie anglaise dress, the hem and puffed sleeves trimmed with red ribbon. He handed it to me and began laying out on the floor lingerie, satin scarves, lace handkerchiefs and a white mantilla. 'Look,' he said, 'my treasure, my solace.' I smiled.

'He whipped me, but he cannot take *them* away from me,' he said.

The Watchman

Jonathan stood by the ledge of the verandah, leaning over between the pots of seed-ferns. Their tendrils shook in the first breeze of the evening and tickled his face. He scratched his face with his smooth hands. If he strained his eyes hard enough, he thought, he would be able to see darkness approaching. Sometimes he thought he could see it.

The darkness.

That's it, like a veil, thin and transparent as the fine net of his mother's black mantilla.

He kept practising this, opening his eyes wider and wider, feeling the strain hurt the sides of his face. Then, a blur.

It was darker, now, but he was not sure that he had seen or understood the approach of darkness.

He stood here at the beginning of every evening, looking out and waiting for the watchman, afraid of the approaching darkness.

The kerosene lamps lit up the village and the barrack-rooms down in the gully, encircling the house on the hill.

The watchman would come with the darkness. He would come with the crunch on the gravel and the smell of woodsmoke from the cooking fires in the village.

Jonathan waited. He watched.

He turned from the ledge of the verandah and saw his mother sitting at her desk behind him, in the drawing-room. Her hands had swollen veins. She was writing, making lists, counting money and closing the business of the day. She looked up at him, *that child*, hanging over the ledge again. Then she smiled. *She* knew.

It was crop time and his father was having a shower. Earlier, he had brought in the smell of burnt cane. He had come up the gap on his horse, then beat the mud off his boots with his switch at the bottom of the verandah steps. When he passed him, he said, 'Waiting, old man?' *He* knew.

There was a crunch on the gravel. Jonathan turned from the ledge with the ferns. He did not want the watchman to see him at the ledge of the verandah looking out for him. But as soon as Jonathan felt that he had put down his things, he would go down the back steps to talk to him.

Sybil, the cook, was by the stove. Theresa, the maid, was folding back the bedspreads and putting down the mosquito nets. They smiled when he passed them. *They* knew. 'Watchman come, eh Jonathan?'

It was now pitch black outside.

The darkness and the watchman had come, and Jonathan marvelled again how his fear had now, suddenly, gone.

The watchman settled down on his green bench at the bottom of the back steps. Jonathan crouched next to him.

It was so dark he could not see the hedge at the other side of the lawn. He felt safe sitting near to the watchman.

The man held a little shoe brush in his large hand. The brush seemed ridiculously small. The action of brushing and shining the shoe with an old piece of cloth, seemed a tiny action in the man's hands against his broad chest. His fingers needed something larger to grasp.

Jonathan stared.

The watchman took care with each task, each small task. He smeared the polish with the piece of cloth, then he brushed vigorously to get the shine up, then more slowly, meditatively. The last action was to rub it all over with a soft cloth. He cleaned the boss's shoes, the madam's and Jonathan's shoes.

The man and the boy did not talk.

After cleaning the shoes, the watchman crossed his legs and rested his chin in his hand, his elbow on his knee. He stared at the ground and then leant back. He took out of his pocket a small parcel of silver

41

paper, folded carefully. It was the inside of an Anchor pack of cigarettes. There were two cigarettes in it. He put one behind his ear and the other he put between his lips. He screwed up the silver paper into a little ball and put it into his pocket. Then he lit the cigarette, cupping it in the palm of his hands to prevent the breeze blowing out the match which he struck with his right hand. He shook the burning match out and flung it in front of him. Then he sat back, stretched and drew a long puff on the cigarette. He inhaled deeply, and blew the smoke into the night. 'Hmm.' That was all he said.

Jonathan listened to his own breathing and the breathing of the watchman. He smelt the sweet tobacco. He noticed the watchman's fingers were still stained with the shoe polish.

Then, Jonathan couldn't stand it any longer. He began to chatter. 'You see that big fire this afternoon, Pompey?'

That was the name Sybil and Theresa called him. Pompey. Jonathan also called him Pompey. Though when he talked to his mother and father, when *they* referred to him, *they* called him 'the watchman'.

When he waited for him, he also thought of him as 'the watchman'.

Pompey nodded, and drew again, a big puff on his cigarette.

'Big, big fire all the way from Diamond, up so, to Golconda. Daddy fighting fire all afternoon, you know.'

'He fighting fire? Hmm, good.'

'Good? Bad. All the cane go burn.'

'All the cane go burn? Good?'

'Pompey, you think that good? Bad, man.'

'Good.' Pompey drew on his Anchor. The cigarette paper frizzelled, the butt got smaller, and the ash grew long and fell on Pompey's knee. He brushed it off. 'Hmm. Good thing!'

Then they fell silent again.

The watchman liked the boy near him, but Jonathan felt that his mind was somewhere else. He had this sense sometimes, after a long silence, that if the watchman spoke it would be so hard that he would have to put his hands over his ears. That was why he would only say 'Hmm', and 'Good'. That was why he kept repeating what he said. But, he repeated things in a way that made Jonathan wonder about what was true. Was it good to burn all the cane down? His father thought it was bad.

The watchman spoke little to Jonathan, but he hardly ever spoke to the boss or the madam. He would nod, which meant, yes. Or, it seemed to.

Jonathan thought that the watchman's voice could break the sound barrier. That was a new idea he had. The sound barrier. He had seen the 'flim' at The Empire theatre in San Andres. *The Breaking of the Sound Barrier*. There was great excitement when his 'pardner' shouted out, 'That's it, they've broken the sound barrier,' as the Canberra jet got to a certain speed. But he had not heard anything. White light. A black and white film.

There was just a hum. Hmm . . .

He expected that he should hear something. 'Nah, man, it invisible, soundless,' his 'pardner' whispered in the packed theatre.

So he felt that the watchman's voice, Pompey's voice, would break the sound barrier. Invisible, soundless. But, *if* he really talked, Jonathan wondered what would happen.

There were a lot of things Jonathan did not understand about the watchman. He did not really understand why Pompey, so silent and strong, should come to his house every evening to polish shoes, run messages for his mother in the 'Chiney', shop, and then watch through the night while he, his mother and father slept.

Sybil said that they called him Pompey, because Pompey was a famous boxer up Princes Town way. 'Pompey? And he was an emperor too, long time, or a general? I see picture about that,' Theresa had joined in once.

Pompey was strong. Tall, black and strong. He was a *blue* black, Mrs Wainwright had once said. There seemed to be admiration, even, in *her* voice.

But then she would also say, 'I don't believe he watches at all. He simply sleeps all night and does another job in the daytime. It's quite wrong that he should be paid anything at all.'

While Jonathan heard this, and a part of him believed it to be true because his mother had said it, he still continued to wonder about Pompey, sitting and walking about patiently, or just standing at the front of the house, watching.

Did he sleep in the daytime?

What did he think about at night when the rest of the earth slept?

Jonathan imagined the night which would be the watchman's companion. Insects, moths around the one electric bulb at the back of the house over the steps, bats swooping back and forth between the house and the almond tree. The night sung.

If Pompey didn't sleep, he didn't dream. Jonathan puzzled on this.

It was the night after. A night of fireflies.

Jonathan was playing dressing-up with his cousin, Gillian. They lit flambeaux and placed them in a circle on the lawn. Venturing out beyond the spill of light, they flirted with the darkness.

The watchman drew his bench nearer to the play of the children, drawn by the excitement of their dance, in and out of the flambeaux which spluttered.

Gillian was disguised in a costume made from one of Mrs Wainwright's old silk evening dresses. She trailed a long black crepe shawl behind her, her young body imitating an older woman's grandeur. Jonathan was beating on a drum made from an old kerosene pan. They were lost in their revelry.

The watchman watched them.

'What those children think they doing? They going and worry that man, yes.' Sybil was looking down from the pantry window. She looked at the watchman. 'He hearing music and seeing dance. They going turn his head. Jonathan, Gillian, what all you doing?' she said aloud.

The children did not hear at first, did not listen.

Suddenly, the watchman stood up and strode out to where the children were dancing and beating the drum. He stood between them, shouting out, 'Maria Montez, Maria Montez.'

Jonathan and his cousin stood still and startled. They were dazed by their music and dance, but also, now, by the suddenness of the watchman's interruption.

They stood and stared. The black shawl dropped from Gillian's bare shoulders.

'Maria Montez, Maria Montez, Maria Montez, the dancing girl!' The watchman laughed, throwing back his head.

Jonathan put his hands over his ears. He could not bear to hear the hard voice of the watchman. The sound barrier.

The yard shook and the darkness trembled.

'All you playing drum and dancing, here in the night with the flambeaux burning. All you know what you doing? Where all you see this kind of thing? All you is children, yes. What all you meddling in, is big people business. My people business.' He took the drum from Jonathan's arms and lifted it up high. He held it up and stroked the top of it with his large hands.

The yard was silent and dark, only a humming noise. Night.

The watchman tapped the drum once, then rested it gently on the grass where there was a light from the flambeaux.

The new moon came out from behind a cloud. A crescent of lime.

'Hmm, all you know my people? My people down in Moruga, where my great-grandfather come from?' The watchman stood tall in the middle of the circle made by the flambeaux.

The darkness outside was thick. The moonlight not reaching the darkness yet.

Jonathan and Gillian crouched and looked up at the watchman. They listened.

'Down in Moruga, when the drum beat, people come together. My grandfather say the people come together, they burn the cane. Now they don't come together. They burn cane, yes, good. But they don't come together. Is you children playing drum. All you don't know what you doing. And me? Meself, watching the night, watching all you property, all you children.' He turned and faced the house as if he was speaking to the house. 'Yes, I watch you. I guard you. I leave the little I have, to guard you against thief in the night. Who tell you, you could trust me?' He turned back to where the children were on the lawn. 'Put out them flambeaux yes, kerosene dangerous. Don't play with fire.'

'You see what I say. He have a memory of that drum, deep inside him. That is we thing.' Sybil turned from the pantry window and pulled Theresa away with her.

'Who is Maria Montez?' Jonathan asked, boldly, the next night.

Jonathan sat next to the watchman on the green bench.

45

The watchman sat with his head pressed into his hands. He raised his head slowly. Jonathan noticed his fingers. They were hands which could make something. He once saw a man in the village, making a cabinet.

The watchman smiled. He looked at Jonathan, hearing the question. *Who is Maria Montez?*

Jonathan snuggled up to the watchman. He smelt the watchman. He smelt of shoe polish and sweet tobacco.

The watchman began to tell a story.

'I leave the house when the dew still on the ground. I take some food by Mistress Maud in the village. I eat some bake, drink some cocoa tea. Next, I take a bath, dress neat and then I catch the bus for San Andres. The bus drop me down by the market in Mucurapo Street. They have three theatres there. Radio City, Gaiety and New Theatre, like a big white palace. You like theatre?' The watchman turned and looked at Jonathan.

'I always sit in the pit. I can't afford house or balcony. I promise meself, I going up there one day. First, there is ten-thirty show, *Escape from Fort Bravo* with Randolph Scott and Maureen O'Hara. I take a little snooze in between when they show the advertisements. The action of the 'flim' right there in my mind. Like daydream *Scaramouche* was the double. Boy, *that* is 'flim', papa. Sword fighting, and woman for so!' The watchman laughed and put his arm round Jonathan's shoulders.

'When I come out into the daylight, it stabbing me right in the eye. I prefer the darkness.

'Before I cross over the road to take in the one-thirty in the Gaiety, I pick up a hops and cheese and a mauby by the parlour.

'Another double. *Vera Cruz* with Sophia Loren. If you see dancing, papa. That woman does dance. Yes, she does dance, but not like Maria. Maria Montez.

'That was when I was real young, you know, young and strong.' Pompey rubbed his right fist in the palm of his left hand. Like he was shining his fist.

'Old 'flim' you know. Black and white. It break down all the time. If you hear noise for so in pit. Men only bawling. Whistling. They just bring the machine from America.

'I forget the title of the 'flim', but I never forget the woman who dance. Sweetness, pure sweetness. And I had me own woman right by me side, you know.' The watchman stared into the darkness, telling the boy the story, but speaking out beyond the boy.

Jonathan listened, rapt. He was looking up at Pompey's face, black like the darkness itself.

The watchman did not talk again.

'What you still doing down here? You should be in bed now. Madam and the boss done finish dinner and I going down. Leave that man alone. You have his head full up with too many things.' Sybil, talked, busy with tidying up.

Jonathan went over the watchman's story. His voice had changed when he said, *Sweetness, pure sweetness. And I had me own woman right by me side.* Pompey had walked into the darkness then, his voice had changed. Hard and soft.

The next evening, Jonathan waited at his post on the verandah ledge. Darkness came, but he could not see its approach. Imperceptibly, it veiled the trees, the canefields, the villages where the kerosene lights came on. No longer could he see the purple horizon.

Then, fire burning up the whole sky.

The noises started. Frogs, moths, beetles.

The watchman did not come. Jonathan was afraid.

The same thing happened again the next night. Darkness came. Fire. No watchman, and he remained afraid.

'Sybil? Where is the watchman? Two nights now he hasn't come.'

'Cheups, why you bothering me, child? And why you bothering yourself? What you 'fraid?'

'Well, he should be here. Maybe, he sick.'

'Jonathan go and play, go and do your homework. You don't have writing and reading to do?'

'But if he sick, he needs a doctor.'

'Doctor, who could afford doctor?'

'Medicine.'

'Medicine! Child go away and stop pestering me.'

'I going to tell mummy and daddy.'

'You think they don't know? Is meself cleaning shoes now. I think tomorrow will be Theresa's turn. Blasted shoes.'

'I'm going to tell them.'

'What they go do?'

'Well . . .'

'Mind your own business, nuh, child.'

Jonathan stayed away from the kitchen. He sat on the verandah listening to his mother and father. They drank rum and sodas. They talked quietly, seriously. After dinner he overheard his mother talking to Sybil.

'What are you saying, Sybil?'

'Is true, madam, that is what they saying.'

'Who is saying, what?'

'People like Mistress Maud. He used to pass by she for food in the morning after he leave here.'

'So?'

'She say, she see people come and take him away. That is what she say. Ambulance come, police.'

Jonathan went over the watchman's story. He felt that Pompey had told him a secret. It had to do with going to the theatre. But, also, there was the way he told his story. The way his voice had changed. Then there was the fact that he didn't sleep or dream. 'Flim' was his dream. Jonathan thought. Then there was the sweetness woman. Now Jonathan thought of it, it sounded as if the watchman wanted to cry. And that was why he walked out into the darkness.

Jonathan questioned Sybil again.

'Sybil, who cooks for Pompey?'

'What you asking me? He must have some woman cooking for him. He looking big and strong.'

'But when does he eat?'

'What you mean? He have the whole day to eat.'

Jonathan looked at Sybil for a sign of something more. Ambulance, police. But she wasn't letting on.

'He have woman to cook for him.' Sybil added.

'Pompey's not married?'

'Jonathan, you come like big people now. What you know?'

Jonathan stared out of the window. He was not satisfied.

'Anyway, what you asking me all these questions for? You looking to get married or something, like them young Indian boy? I go find a nice little black girl for you to marry with. She go make you feel nice. But madam not going to like that.' Sybil laughed. She lifted Jonathan up, big as he was, and hugged him. 'You get a lot loving, yes.' Jonathan squirmed to release himself from her arms.

'Is only you mother you like to kiss you and give you hug up now that you think you is a big man. And Pompey is you friend.' Jonathan broke away.

Sybil looked out of the window into the darkness. 'You think I can't go mad too, leaving me children for this blasted work. I bet you is he burning the estate down.'

Jonathan overheard his father. 'He'll be looked after. I don't think we should interfere.'

'I feel we should do something.'

'You can't interfere. They have their ways.'

No one spoke to Jonathan. They could see him waiting and watching. They knew why.

'So, it was because she left him?' Mrs Wainwright spoke to Sybil.

'Yes, madam, she leave long time. The neighbour used to come and clean out for him. Everybody know. He leave Esperance Village and come and live down Diamond way. He get a room there in some back street. That's no way for a man to live. Up Esperance is where he get the name Pompey. He was a boxer, you know, like the real Pompey. But he didn't even used to go by the rum shop self, in Diamond. But news follow him. All the fellas know she leave him. They say she dancing in one them club down by the wharf, where fishermen and oil men does go pay day. That is why the watchman work suit him, something to do in the night.'

'What should we do, Sybil?'

'Madam, what you asking me? I don't know.'

'But he's one of yours, Sybil.'

'Madam, what you saying?'

'Maybe I could send him some egg custard?'

Sybil turned away. 'Egg custard? He don't know what that is now. His mind gone away. They say he only shouting out one thing. One thing alone whirling about in that proud head of his. Maria Montez! Maria Montez! The dancing girl. They say he does take anything and beat it.'

Jonathan could hear the watchman's voice. He whispered, 'Pompey.' He looked out into the darkness, over the barrack-rooms and the village. He searched the darkness trying to understand.

There was another fire.

'Pompey.'

Maria Montez . . . sweetness, pure sweetness . . . Jonathan heard his voice in the breeze coming over the canefields.

Sybil muttered, angrily. 'Egg custard? Egg custard my arse!'

Ballad for the New World

The snapshot in the old family album shows an all-American-kinda-looking guy. We were in the shadow of America a long time, a long time. '. . . rum and Coca-Cola . . . working for the Yankee dollar.'* Nineteen forties, nineteen fifties, the decades get mixed up: Jitterbug, Rock-and-Roll at the Empire Cinema, the Globe, Radio City 12.30, Rivoli in Coffee Street San Fernando.

Hollywood.

Was there anything for him then? His mother took him out of school. He worked the boats at night: Import/Export down by the wharf. Did he have a time? I wanted to know, to trace the regret, the anger, the wish to die – young.

The snapshot shows him in white T-shirt, beige slacks. Were they T-shirts then? and slacks? We called them pants. They called them pants too. (The Americans.) He was slim with short hair like young guys now: fresh-faced, frightened, looking brave and startled; looking for a new world. Dark. He lifted weights. The white T-shirt tight at the muscles on his arms. He rode a motor-bike. I, small, rode pillion fast down the pond stretch with the wind and him and my arms around his waist. He had a dog, Mutt, from the *Mutt and Jeff* comic strip; a squirrel all day long in his pocket, on his shoulder, running over his neck, nuzzling in his chest. He had a parrot in a cage on the back verandah. One day, it flew off to the swamp and didn't come back. Next to his bed he had other cages with two rabbits, an agouti and a small mongoose. He rode horses out of the sugar-cane estate yard, cantering the traces with Baboolal, the young East

*Lord Invader 'Rum and Coca-Cola' 1943.

51

Indian boy. He used to lie on top of his bed, on top of the counterpane with his arms behind his head cocked on the pillows, thoughtful, looking at his menagerie on the sill of the Demerara window with one leg drawn up and the other lying out. Resting, he dreamt of horses in the dawn with Baboolal.

When he started lifting weights he began to broaden. In this other snapshot he is definitely short next to his taller brother and his even taller friend, but here on the steps of the bungalow with Mutt he is the all-American-kinda-looking guy.

We weren't American or English. We were French creoles. But – that was fading away. That was fading away fast in the yellow and wrinkled faces of the aunts and uncles embayed in the wickerwork chairs on the wide verandahs who talked of the 'good old days', those old-time days in the cocoa hills. And, now they say, 'When cocoa was king', looking at the state of the island, hardly even remembering. Nowadays some of the children from the families marry coloured people and people who aren't Catholic.

Independence was in the air.

Independence had always been in the air, was always in the air. Not the open-door-the-British-Foreign-Secretary-held-open-kinda independence. No.

Freedom

Riot

   and

Affray

Stamping feet on the asphalt-pitch road.

'What is that noise? Shut the door, girl. Close the windows.'

That noise on the other side of the fence we were trying to shut out.

And, we had had the war too. It had come and gone: Germans, Japs. Black guys went to war for King and Country far away, white fellas too. The West Indian Regiment. Now we've got war memorials like exclamation marks. I remember a pink dirty crushed ration card on the shelf in the pantry which we had to show the commisserie man to get sugar, rice and coconut oil. In the streets the calypsonians were singing 'Chiney never had a VJ Day', and in dark places where the sun shone hot and strong, in red dirt back yards with governor plum trees, music came from dustbin covers, and oil drums were fashioned and tempered in that same fire behind the fence we were trying to put out.

Now I think of it no one ever told me when I was small, smaller than him in the snapshot, that six million people had been gassed by civilised Europeans. Only, on Good Friday, at the Mass of the Pre-Sanctified, we said special prayers for the conversion of pagans, heretics and Jews. And, during the Stations of the Cross, I wondered why the Barbadians had nailed Jesus to the cross.

On the radio in the drawing-room: 'Hiroshima . . . Nagasaki . . .'

'We will have to pay for this,' his mother said when she heard the news. 'We'll have to pay for this.' Hiroshima, Nagasaki. Far away headlines in *The Gazette*.

We were in the shadow of America a long time, a long time. Like under a big umbrella. '. . . rum and Coca-Cola . . . working for the Yankee dollar'.

You see, you start telling the story about a guy and then you get to telling the story of a time, a place, a people and a world. Then I start getting into the story. Well I made that choice early. I remember him well, the all-American-kinda-looking guy on the steps of the sugar-cane estate bungalow with Mutt his dog. Broad shouldered, his stare holds Baboolal: the white French creole with the Indian boy.

It was one night out on the sugar estate . . .

He was still at home, lifting weights under the house in the afternoon. He was the last of the boys to leave home. That's what she (my, and his mother, she who said, 'We will have to pay for this') always said: 'He was the last of the boys to leave home', with that look in her eyes which knew that we all had to go eventually and leave her alone with her husband. It wasn't true that he had been the last of the boys to leave. I was. But for her there were always the boys, my sister and me. So, he was the last of the boys to leave. Then she had me to speak to, had me there, not like a child but more like a lover, a changeling companion, a mirror, a fairy child, a Peter Pan – but that's another tale. Then I left and she and her husband were alone and she was always wanting us to come back, looking out of the window down the gravel road. He always did, dropping in with the jitney to do a message, carrying something, have a coffee with her at the edge of the dining-room table, pulled by her, she listening, reaching out to touch his arm on the table with raised veins, listening, feeling proud. When he came, there would have to be a leg of lamb and macaroni pie. She wouldn't have siesta if he was going to drop in for tea, or might. She would bake a sponge cake and be tired in the evening and have to have a whisky and soda. He would have a slice of the cake for her sake between cigarettes and black coffee, not tea. She would look at him with half a look of owning and half a look of relinquishing and then call him over to the side of the drawing-room to have a talk about his job. He marvelled, we all did, how she could talk of cars and mechanics when it was cars and mechanics, and later about oil derricks, bits, blow outs and cementing. Then she would let him go to his father on the verandah. She liked the idea that her boys were close to their father. It was just an idea. The man said little and the boys were left yearning and looking elsewhere, dreaming the dream of their ancestors, El Dorado. His memory was the dawn, horses and Baboolal.

. . . But maybe it was on one of those nights when he had already left home and there was a leg of lamb and macaroni pie. Out of the blue he bet me I would not run down into the yard in the dark, down behind the hibiscus hedge into the savannah and touch the trunk of the big silk cotton tree under which a coolie man was buried and a jumbie lived. If I did he would take me to the pictures there and then, night-time pictures there and then, that night. He bet it not as a threat or something to demean me, that I might not be able to do, but rather as a warm reaching-out challenge to my boyish youth and his own, spoken across the wide polished oval dining-room table like a mirror for us to see ourselves and the servants passing out and coming in through the pantry door when my mother rang the little brass bell. He spoke it with affection and warmth and with an endless desire for adventure. 'Come, boy, let we go.' He wanted me to have an adventure and he wished to be the one to offer it. I leapt out of my chair and went out into the dark, not pretending, through the hibiscus hedge, across the gravel road, down into the gully and the savannah to the base and trunk of the silk cotton tree where the coolie man was buried and my heart jumping for the jumbie that might be. I touched the tree. I did what he had said and ran all the way back up to the bungalow, up the back steps, through the pantry. There, I had done it, and off, at once, because we were late and my mother said that we wouldn't make it on time. We went to the cinema. Theatre.

Time would stop for us in the jitney round the bend by Palmiste where the bull gouged out the overseer's stomach in the savannah, over the potholed roads, through the kerosene flambeaux-lit villages, through the dark to the Gaiety Theatre in Mucurapo Street, warm and alive with talk, car horns, roast corn, peanuts and channa from vendors with tin stands lit by flambeaux burning through perforated holes made with an ice pick in an old biscuit tin. Palms warm with hot groundnuts in small brown-paper bags, throwing the shells on the ground. Night-time theatre.

My memories kept by a memory of him. I longed for him on a horse, held in front, too small to straddle the strong back, to rub those sweating flanks, with him and Baboolal's thin brown legs flying in the wind.

It was a double: *The Wild One* with Marlon Brando, and *Rebel Without a Cause* with James Dean. Looking at the snapshot it is James Dean who was always young that I remember. I remember his chiselled cheek bones, his sad soft eyes dreaming of an early death: and him in the snapshot, his sad soft eyes, sitting with Mutt on the steps of the bungalow.

They were all of a time, mixed up in memory. A decade of heroes and gods. Brando, James Dean and a little later Elvis. He of the snapshot liked Frank Sinatra, and Frankie Laine singing 'I believe'. Singing, 'I believe in every drop of rain that falls', and 'When you hear a new-born baby cry, I believe'. Mario Lanza's 'Ave Maria'. He tried to crack the glass in the bathroom window like him when he took a shower.

We weren't American, but we lived in the shadow of America a long time, a long time . . . 'Working for the Yankee dollar'.

Hiroshima, Nagasaki. Like a big parasol.

'They will have to pay for this,' she said.

Yes, gods: Brando, Dean. The way they walked. They way they talked. Bigger than life on the big screen: John Wayne, Errol Flynn, Rock Hudson, heroes of the 12.30 matinée. Heroes for him in the snapshot, for the black tess on the pavement, the badjohn on the sidewalk under the rum shop. Like them he had an odyssey weaving the gravelled traces with his motor-bike, skidding the corners at the Wallerfield American Base Camp in the motor-car rally on two

55

wheels, the white promise of the carnival-queen beauty-show cat walk screaming at the curb, shaking their pony tails.

Twice they woke her, madonna mother, prayer of rosaries and novenas for her boys all night, while her husband snored forgetting that he had begotten sons. In the next room in the troubled house her débutante daughter asleep under the picture of guardian angels set in battle array. Twice they woke her, his pardner messenger at the front door with the news. His car was in the ravine. He had been snatched from death, tugged to life with a string of rosary beads, whispered novenas and ejaculations to Saint Christopher.

She had kept on believeing; so had he.

'He is a religious boy. He has a natural religious feeling. He always prays. Always thinking of God. The Man Upstairs he calls Him. If I think of any of my boys being religious I think of him. He used to wake early and take me to the First Friday morning mass. He always had his rosary in his pocket. He had a strong sense of right and wrong. Always went to confession and communion, a religious boy, pious. Used his missal.'

That was her creed. Although they always, the boys, followed mass from the back porch of the church and smoked cigarettes during the sermon leaning up against their cars in the church yard. But, they were the boys. I, blent with her in prayer, kneeling side by her under the statue of Saint Thérèse of Lisieux, The Little Flower. Taking it all in.

You try to put it all down before it passes away. Sing the ballad for the heroes of the new world. Heroes of the dawn, he and Baboolal.

Do you remember that James Dean walk? The way he kicked a stone in *East of Eden*? The way he hung his head and the way he suddenly bounded out of himself up the stairs to find his mysterious mother? The way he would hold back, hang back in there, inside himself with his sad soft eyes dreaming of an early death, and then hit out, want to hit someone, hit himself, pound the ribs of the house with his fists? He was like that, a badjohn. He had to hit someone. He would have to cuff someone down.

There was this mixture in him of sadness and softness, tenderness and hardness all blent in one, this religious boy who was the last of the boys to leave home. I see him now, he begins to change '. . . rum and Coca-Cola . . . working for . . . the Yankee dollar.' Grog.

56

White shirt, collar and tie when he used to sell motor-cars in San Fernando for his uncle. He quit that. He had to make more money. He had to prove himself otherwise he would have to hit somebody. Big car time.

Cocoa and sugar dead. Motor-cars
oil
the decades pass.

Now Texaco is written where the British Oil Company used to be. The history book says they sucked the orange dry.

Later in his khaki pants, unshaven, bare-backed, brow stained, smelling of cigarettes and black coffee, rum, his hands smelling of oil, we would go for a drive alone to see where he worked. Alone, driving through the bush to the clearing in the forest where the oil well stood, the derrick pumping out oil, piping stacked on the sides. I learnt about drilling a hole, cementing, bits, blow outs, and the whole adventure, the whole far-flung adventure of his – American, British, French, Dutch, Spanish here again for El Dorado the sixteenth-century myth.

There was no stopping him. He said it himself, 'I am a self-made man.' He still liked to ride his motor-bike for the hell of it, back from the beach with a carnival queen riding pillion in the dusk, in the amber of the dusk and rum. Madonna mother prayed all the while for him and the parish priest came to bless the office when he formed his own company and hanged the picture of 'The Sacred Heart' over his desk.

He went from there to become a millionaire. He made himself, he said, and said it again, 'I'm a self-made man,' forgetting (if he ever knew) what whiteness meant. What did it cost him? He had collected houses, cars, companies, registered companies.

The story begins to fade as I begin to lose him as he enters dreams, his hallucinations, *folies de grandeur*, the old madness of the ancestors of the savannahs of Monagas, the pampas of Bolivar. They dreamt of horses and the building of large houses and eternal gardens, dreaming of a grandeur they thought they once had.

He lost his James Dean rebel smile. His broad shoulders caved in. His sad soft eyes stared blindly without anger or dreams.

'If only Baboolal could see me now. If only Baboolal could see me now . . . If only he could see this lake with ice, this land with conifers,' (the dream of Christmas in a tropic mind). 'Baboolal never see ice, except he see it by the USE ICE factory San Fernando roundabout, or shave ice on the promenade.'

It all came rushing back, this ballad for the heroes of the new world as we sat in a little Spanish restaurant in the old world.

'I going away,' he said.

'Go to a hot country,' I said.

'Maybe hot, maybe cold,' he said.

I paid the cheque (unusually) for the last time.

As he stares now through amber at the green dream of green canefields in the sun, he remembers the East Indian boy Baboolal barebacked with him on horses cantering the gravelled traces.

If Baboolal could see him now, I thought.

'. . . rum and Coca-Cola, down Point Cumana . . . working for the Yankee Dollar.'

The Question of the Keskidee

Cecile Monagas could not understand this way of dying. There was a kind of impropriety about it: the way Philip had woken early before the birds and before the sun had freshened the room still smelling of sleep. She had heard him get up and, knowing that his death was expected, had herself got up and followed him into the kitchen where she found that he had helped himself to a beer from the fridge and was drinking it slowly from the neck of the bottle while gazing on to the blank walls of the courtyard. She did not say anything. Half an hour later he called, ringing the bell on his bedside table. The keskidees were already chattering in the calabash tree under his window, asking their questions.

'Cecile, I am dying, call the priest. Tell him to bring notepaper.' In the first days when the family had lived at the ancient city of San Jose de Orunya there had been no paper to be found on the island. People forgot things because they were accustomed to them being written down. Much suffering and cruelty was buried, then. But in these present days of improper deaths the last of the Monagas could cry for paper and pen, even ink. Not like the time when a searcher after El Dorado had emptied all the ink into the Orinoco. Cecile provided notepaper and arranged it on the bedside table with a fountain pen and a bottle of Quink ink, together with a bowl of water and a linen hand-towel.

The impropriety continued when Cecile heard her brother-in-law, Philip Monagas, go down to the kitchen again to help himself to another beer. Her daughters, his nieces, were beginning to rustle in their linen sheets. They were unaware of the announcement of death. Her husband was in his study looking at his stamps through a magnifying glass. He seemed unperturbed and told Cecile to go ahead, 'Call the priest.' Because the telephones were not working, Cecile wrote a note to her sister which she gave to the market-cart man, Ramdass, to deliver. In it she asked her to come and help. Her sister knew the whole story of which this was the end.

1

To all the lodgers at Miss Nivet's boarding house at the top of Chancery Lane he had been the 'English gentleman'. Since his return to the island he would sit on the verandah in the evenings wearing a grey flannel suit with a starched white collar and cuffs. In the morning he wore white linen, a straw hat, and carried an umbrella. He used white, pressed linen handkerchiefs which had lain on the shelves of cedar presses in sachets of cuscus grass from Dominica. He had the manners of an English gentleman of the late Victorian or early Edwardian period. His hair was always well trimmed, well combed, and he displayed a restrained politeness at all times.

Miss Nivet, who had told his mother that she would look after him well, remembered him as a boy when he had lodged with her before he had left the island and gone away to England. The other lodgers and members of the household, particularly the daughters of Miss Nivet, and the maids in the pantry who giggled, hiding their faces behind their fingers, also remembered him well. He had not been like the other young boys who 'knocked about town', as the daughters would say, dressed in muslin with ribboned hair sitting in the wickerwork chairs.

'He's always scribbling,' Miss Nivet said to Mrs Monagas. 'Giselle, my dear. You don't mind me calling you Giselle, since we were in the convent together?'

'Scribbling?' Mrs Monagas looked at Miss Nivet. 'Philippe, scribbling?' Mrs Monagas looked at Miss Nivet again. She had always been told that Miss Nivet was slightly coloured, the wrong Nivet, some grandfather up on the estates and then all these other Nivets began popping up with crinkly hair and marmoset eyes. 'Of course, call me Giselle, after all we were in the same class with Mother Gertrude of the Five Wounds, you remember?'

'Yes, the maids have noticed him in the Botanical Gardens,

scribbling. He walks about with a notebook and takes the horticultural names of the trees and shrubs. Also, Kamina, the little coolie girl I have to help the maid, found a little black notebook on the back verandah. It had recorded conversations between Kamina and Ram the yardboy.'

'It's the exams? Those priests? It's true. He acts strange at times.'

'Not at all, Giselle. He is charming and he's got beautiful table manners.'

'Well his father will have to speak to him. It's the mathematics and the sciences, or the priesthood.'

'So, my boy, you haven't told me yet, McBride & Plummer or Jones & McFarland – which is it to be? Difficult to choose, I can see. Both excellent firms with high standards and impeccable reputations.'

'I don't know, Papa.' His son's indecision irritated Mr Monagas.

Chartered Accountancy were hallowed words whispered on the verandahs of the avenues and the boulevards.

'You could do a year with McBride & Plummer. I will see old George Plummer. He will give you a place in the office. I will see him at bridge this afternoon down at the club. I've done enough favours for him.'

'Whatever you say, Papa.'

'You're sure you don't want to be a priest? Father Gormally says that you are a very devout acolyte and now the Archbishop is trying to encourage young local boys to think of a vocation. Your mother would be so pleased.'

'I'll have to think about it, Papa.'

And so talk of Philip's career circulated round the family.

'Philip is going to be a chartered accountant.'

'Philip?'

'Philippe Monagas, Giselle's last boy, her Felipo, imagine.'

'Not a priest?' Aunt Louise asked. 'Poor Giselle. We had hoped for a priest, the first mass and the newly ordained's blessing, kissing the consecrated fingers.'

'No, but a chartered accountant, my dear. He will do so well. He will be a fine young man when he comes back.' Aunt Ursule had distinguished herself in mathematics at the convent, to the consternation of her brothers, and hated the eternity of the morning: embroidery, mending and beating whites of egg with granulated sugar for meringues which the uncles loved so much.

'My dear, a chartered accountant, how wonderful!' Aunt Nini always succumbed to Aunt Ursule. 'With McBride & Plummer, an English firm.'

Philip was to take a secret with him to England, a glimmer of which had been glimpsed by Mildred, the maid, when she had discovered him investigating and copying down Latin, horticultural notations for the cocorite, banyan and palmiste in the Botanical Gardens; remembering Charles Kingsley's 'doric columns of ancient Greece' first seen at Aripo, but now growing in the shadow of the Governor's grey stone house.

Other fragments of Philip's secret lay buried in the weekly compositions which Father Gormally had so much admired and his own father discouraged, preferring him to spend his time with theorems, logarithms and mathematical problems, to train his brain for the computations in the service and the management of capital. 'Be a priest if not an accountant, my boy.'

The compositions were written neatly in sky blue Quink ink along aquamarine lines on white paper mottled with bagasse splinters between the royal blue covers of a copy-book with the king's head in an oval frame. Father Gormally had chosen his subjects well to stimulate his young charges. Philip was particularly attached to the last composition in the book, 'Sounds', a description of sounds resonant in childhood: rain on shingle; wind in the dry season whispering through Casaurinas; the swish of serrated leaves in the canefields; the rush of brown water in muddy canals, the drip of rain in the cocoa; the thunder of waves; the rattle of pods on the dry flamboyant trees in flame and the question of the keskidee, the golden inhabitor of gardens, cocoa plantations, savannahs and forest clearings on the island and the continent; the questioner of the morning, putting the question, 'Qu'est-ce qu'il dit?' with an irritating persistence which was to become more insistent in Philip's later life.

All the family went down to the wharf to wish him farewell and to see him off on the *Santa Elena*. Josephine the cook, Mildred the maid and Kamina her assistant, together with Ram the yardboy and Olga the washer and ironer, all came out on to the front verandah in their best clothes to wish the boy well. They stood in the background, or just to the side, as the family stood on the verandah steps for a family portrait which Mr Simonet from the Long Circular in Belmont always came to take on different occasions, setting up his contraption, rickety on the gravel. 'Smile please.'

All the family went on board: the parents, brothers and sisters, aunts and uncles, grandparents and numerous cousins. His mother had packed into his trunk among the well-labelled shirts and handkerchiefs and linen, zaboca, bottles of guava jelly, sugar cakes, toulum, guava cheese and other delicacies of his school days. All smelt sweet between layers of cuscus grass and there was a bottle of eau-de-Cologne.

Philip watched the island grow smaller. He stood on the deck looking back as they moved slowly out from the gulf: past the archipelago of the 'Five Islands', Gasparilo, Monos with its Red Howlers; Pointe Baleine, the old whaling station; Huevos past the bocas; moving towards the Dragon's Mouth and the Venezuelan Peninsular. He remembered his holidays 'down the islands'; his butterfly net; picking the virgin orchids, the epiphytes, a word he learnt from Aunt Ursule who had also told him of an ancient aunt she admired who had made an expedition to the upper reaches of the Orinoco. He remembered putting out his fishing line from the side of a perogue and swinging in the hammocks in the evening.

The sun was an orange ball on the invisible coastline of Venezuela. He remembered his fear of the remous as he looked down at the black water. He looked ahead with a breeze in his face and a salt, spray drizzle in his eyes. When he looked back, the sun had sunk and all that he loved went out.

But, alone on the ocean, he thought of the alternatives which he had escaped. He did not know what was going to happen. He was relieved that he had escaped the destinies of his brothers: football and cricket clubs for the fathers and sons of fathers on every interminable afternoon, the game dictated by the season; he had escaped business associations and church sodalities. No longer would he have to endure endless weekends with cousins and more cousins, trapped 'down the islands' in the fairy-tale houses of Windermere, Avalon, Copper Hole and Marielva with aunts and uncles playing bridge. He had escaped the afternoons at the club and the evenings at cousins' homes, on the verandahs with aunts who talked of death and sickness and uncles who boasted about their exploits at hunting and selling merchandise.

He would miss his mother because she was his mother and he would miss Josephine, Mildred and Kamina, yes, Olga and Ram too. He would miss the talk and excitement of the back verandah. He would miss the light. He would miss the green mountains and the flowering shrubs and trees in the Botanical Gardens; the sea and the pebbles on the beach.

He wondered about England and whether it had its terrors: the terror of church on a Good Friday afternoon; the company of widows and widowers; the repetition of the rosary, confession, novenas; the claustrophobia of eau-de-Cologne and talcum powder; the fluttering of muslin curtains in the evenings and the barking of dogs at night waking him from hot dreams.

Lastly, he thought, whispering it to himself, looking over the railings down at the black water, 'I've escaped weddings and christenings.' He would not have to be a godfather or be the prey of the mothers of the debutantes.

He had packed his little notebooks and bought himself a dictionary which his mother thought was a missal because it looked like a prayer book or the Bible when he was packing it.

2

Philip eventually settled in London, boarding on the Edgware Road, recommended by distant cousins. He tried to erase the lilt in his voice, the English mistaking him for being Welsh or Mediterranean.

'How about a pint at "The Flask", Monagas?'

'No thanks old chap, got to shift this work.' He learnt accepted expressions which allowed him to decline invitations without sounding rude or awkward. Consequently, he led a solitary life, finding his conversations with strangers sitting in parks, or through a recognised affinity later shared over a cup of tea at the Lyons Corner House, after looking at paintings in the National Gallery.

One night he dreamt that he was trying to write a story but the ink did not flow from the pen and the white sheets kept fading away into the writing desk. Aunt Ursule had set off on an expedition of the Orinoco to collect the ink which had been deposited there in a former century.

The years passed with his mother writing from time to time: 'Dear Felipo, your father wants to know what is happening?' He had passed his exams and was now a chartered accountant but he refused to return to the island and persuaded McBride & Plummer to keep him at the office in London. His brothers said it was nonsense and that he should return to do a good day's work and make some money; business was thriving and there was lots of money to make from the newly developing oil industry. Young men were journeying off to the oil lake in Maracaibo's El Dorado. 'He can't just hang on in London, visiting art galleries, museums, theatres, and reading poetry hoping to write one day.' The voices of his brothers came across the ocean.

The war saved Philip. He was trapped in Europe. The *Santa Elena*, one of the main ships of the line which went to the island, was torpedoed off Vigo and his mother wrote to say that Aunt Bijou and Uncle Carl had gone down with her.

But, later, on the Continent, Philip was unprepared for the transformation which was to take place in his perceptions: in the reawakening of his memory by the light of the Impressionists; Gauguin's beach at Saint Pierre in Martinique with the trees like sea-grapes and the manchineel at Manzanilla, blue, ochre and rusty barks; the rotting hull of a fishing boat; the procession of women, the marchandes in coloured cottons and muslin; a young coconut tree; a wild goat; a fisherman and a brown-skinned lady sitting on a stool and reading a book. He heard again the cries of the cigale in the eucalyptus trees, the crackle of dry leaves in the dusty hedges. He was astonished to find the pink coral of the oleander and the vermilion bougainvillaea. Women reminded him of his mother and aunts. Gentlemen were like his father and he felt at home, strangely, with the movement of their hands when they spoke; something the English had made him embarrassed about. They sat on promenades, or on the balconies of houses whose colonial replicas he remembered with jalousies, verandahs hung with ferns and palms in pots.

First in Chartres and then at Notre Dame and later in the churches of Seville and Madrid he asked himself where were these civilising forces of beauty when they landed on the beaches of Moruga. In the palaces and churches fretted with the gold of the Incas and the silver of the Aztecs he understood the meaning of genocide. He heard Rimbaud's voice, 'My race has never risen, except to plunder.' In a dream that night he saw Uncle Carl and Uncle Pierre by the wharf near the lighthouse. He smelt copra sweating and the syrup of crushed cane and there was an unending procession of black people leaping off high cliffs into the sea.

The more he thought about the island, its history, geography, topography and geology which he had researched in the British Museum, spurred on by the insistence of fate to an exact knowledge of the place, he was encouraged to return to save himself and to write a story. He smiled when he thought to himself, an answer to the keskidee's 'Qu'est-ce qu'il dit?' He returned to his old notebooks.

3

He returned home to find that his father had lost his memory. 'You remind me of a son I had who went away. What happened to him?' He turned to his wife to ask the question. Later his father died with his mother following in sympathy.

Miss Nivet's boarding house still existed, except that now it was managed by her middle daughter Janine, who had not married. 'Terribly selfish of these men,' Miss Nivet said to Philip, looking at him and seeing that any hope which she had had in the sweet young boy with beautiful table manners was now quite diminished. Her other two daughters had succeeded in marrying, one to a Portuguese merchant, which confirmed Mrs Monagas' view years later that they were still the wrong Nivet. The youngest, Marguerite, had done herself proud and married an English officer from the Fleet Air Arm. 'There was no knowing what these young English lads would do when they got out here,' was the view from the twittering verandahs.

Ram, Kamina, Olga and Mildred had left. They used to come back from time to time to visit old 'Madam' but it was a long time since anyone had seen them. The new servants did not stay long and now they wanted to be called domestic workers. His cousins had married and produced equally large families as their parents. Some of the girls had become nuns and the boys priests. Mad men and women were roaming the streets, the asylum was overflowing, so the families sent their deranged to institutions in Canada and England. Recently Julie, a young girl 'from one of the families', had been sent to England with religious mania, believing that she had received the stigmata and complaining of bleeding every month. Aunt Ursule who was now ninety-six refused to do any more sewing or embroidery. 'It is my eyes, dear, I can hardly see.' But Philip remembered that she had always hated the mornings of sewing and the making of meringues for the uncles. Despite her reputedly bad sight she spent her time doing crosswords and playing patience, sitting on a rocker near to the ledge with the angelhair fern which reminded her of her grandmother.

Philip's brothers were in business and their stature kept reminding him of portraits of Pizzaro and Cortes he had seen in the Prado. He felt himself to be an anachronism sitting on Miss Nivet's verandah. What he remembered was fast disappearing and before it should completely fade he needed to write his story. But the more he consulted his notebooks with their horticultural, historical, geographical, topographical and geological notations, the more he felt unequal to the task. He even went back to his childhood compositions, seeking instruction in the art. He kept asking himself what he had been given, what he had been left, and increasingly he felt it to be an inheritance of cruelty. His research creaked beneath the burden of history and the necessity for an artistry, no examples of which had been bequeathed him by his ancestors. He now knew that his secret was as old as the Spanish Armada; as old as the discovery of the New World when the three galleons, the *Nina*, the *Pinta* and the *Santa Maria* lay adrift in the Serpent's Mouth crowded with the outcasts of Europe kneeling and thanking the Holy Trinity for land.

He moved to his brother and sister-in-law's house. There he grew older, pursuing his art secretly. No one knew what he was doing, but the story went about that he was inventing something; a rumour started by his brothers because they hoped to patent some useful machine, but distrusted those hopes in Philip, nothing so profitable.

The days had an even pattern to them: breakfast with the birds out on the terrace above the orange and grapefruit trees overlooking the gulf; then a stroll down into the town, shaded by his umbrella, down the one hundred and fifty steps past the parlour, above which Miss Redhead trained young girls as stenographers on new machines from

67

America. He would rest under the parlour for a while and indulge a childhood taste for sour sweets, always embarrassed because his tongue went so red from sucking them. The neat girls from the convent with slender waists pulled in with belts and their hair pressed down with oil, smiled to see the gentleman with the red tongue under the umbrella. Philip would stroll on, fascinated by the click of the typewriters; reminding him of beetles and cicadas, while he imagined the newly acquired skills of the young stenographers' fingers and the sentences which popped up in front of them on the pristine, white sheets. He envied the clarity of their compositions.

People passed him as he stood under a lamppost in the shade of his umbrella. At first they used to remark, 'Eh, eh, look at that white gentleman under a parasol,' but it did not take long for familiarity to create invisibility, though a white gentleman, dressed as an Edwardian in a white linen suit, standing under an umbrella in Cipero Street, was unusual. It was unique. But he became known to the vendors of pistache and morning newspapers, and most particularly to Miss Thomas, the Presbyterian, Indian seamstress who sewed for his sister-in-law and her sister and had rooms under the office of McBride & Plummer, where he still went on mornings to check papers. 'Good morning to you, Miss Thomas.'

'Good morning, Mr Monagas. You early today?'

'I don't think so, Miss Thomas, not by the church clock.'

'You does go to that church, you is a Catholic? I is a Presbyterian, but they say is the same God. I join them for the education. They going and give my son a scholarship to go away.'

'You want your son to go away, Miss Thomas?'

'How you mean sir? He go get a profession – doctor, lawyer, like you sir and you is an accountant? They have nothing for him here, sir. But he go come back and help he mother.'

'I see, I see, I wish him all the luck in the world. Once he goes away . . .' Philip's voice trailed away as he began to ascend the stairs to his office.

'Pardon sir, what you say?'

'You sound like a keskidee, Miss Thomas.' Philip laughed. 'Once he goes away he may not want to come back, but he will miss the good weather.' Then he turned and looked at her. 'Will he study history, do you think?'

'History? The weather, you like the sun, eh sir?'

Philip reached the top of the stairs and Miss Thomas followed him up, sweeping the steps as she climbed them. 'The light, the light.'

'Eh heh? Let me sweep these steps down properly.'

Then it began to happen more frequently that he did not go down to the office, but stayed up at the house, having the papers sent up to him, spending his mornings and sometimes most of the day on the terrace overlooking the gulf and having his meals brought to him on a tray.

Young suitors pursuing his nieces would come out on to the terrace and wanting to be jolly so as to ease their shyness with the old man, would say, 'How's the invention, Uncle Philip?'

At first he would not even acknowledge their presence, and then suddenly he would turn on them, 'What did you say, young man?' The young men would beat a fast retreat, offering a mumbled excuse, not being able to muster the courage to frame another question.

Consequently, he got the reputation for being quite severe with his young nieces and nephews who used to come and play in the grapefruit trees on the bank below the terrace, which was where the keskidees flocked to chatter and ask their questions, which the children imitated to try and confuse the birds. Then the children, because nothing passed their ears when the grown-ups were talking, would cry out in unison, 'Uncle Philip, how's the invention?' He continued reading or pretended to ignore them. There was a macaw in a cage on the terrace which had been taught to say 'good morning', and to repeat things which people said, so one's voice always had an echo. The children imitating the keskidee, and the macaw all other voices, created an absurd babel.

Occasionally he used to put on one of the records which he had brought with him from England – Mozart's Horn Concerto – which gave a sense of elation as he watched the birds of the morning rise and fall in the valley with the blue woodsmoke. Then he would drift off, feeling tired.

'Qu'est-ce qu'il dit?' asked the keskidees.

He shrieked inside of himself, 'Nothing.'

When he looked up to his sister-in-law's bedroom window he invariably saw her at the windowsill, writing. 'Cecile, what are you writing?'

She would answer, 'This and that; my diary. Would you like some lemonade?'

'A diary?' He saw in the eyes of her daughters and herself the signs of a pilgrimage.

'Good night Uncle Philip,' his nieces swooped on to the terrace, their crinolines in a whirl; 'off to a dance at the club.' They kissed him goodnight. He enjoyed the affection and was affectionate in turn; instructing Cecile to let him have the chauffeur on an afternoon to take him into the town to de Lima's, where he would buy little silver, filigree, bon-bon dishes as presents, or bouquets and chocolates.

'Father Sebastian is here to hear your confession.' The household were surprised how often Father Sebastian used to come now. They would peep out on to the terrace and watch the two men sitting next to each other, talking, or just staring. To Cecile it seemed an unusual way of hearing confession.

One night he woke and called Cecile by ringing the bell on the bedside table. 'I can hear singing.' He had been dreaming of the singing voices in the forests of San Raphael.

'No one is singing, Philip, and the girls are back from the dance, safe in bed.' Cecile put out the light. She had been waiting up for her daughters; guiding their way home with decades of the rosary. The softest stirring in the house woke her, since she slept between dreams and the expectation of tragedy.

'They were massacred,' he called after her; trying to pull the mosquito net from under the mattress in order to get out of the bed, and then changing his mind. He fell back on to the pillows to dream of orchids blooming on the graves of the massacred.

'I think Philip is dying,' Cecile had said to her husband when she got back into bed. She said it to herself because her husband slept soundly, unaware of his wife's nocturnal vigils; guessing at them from the black circles he saw under her eyes the following day.

So it was just like her to hear her brother-in-law go down to the kitchen at dawn, where she found him drinking a bottle of beer from the neck and then announcing his imminent death and the need to see Father Sebastian. 'He is hearing the angels, Father, I should come quickly.' The telphone crackled.

70

Having alerted the family to the expected death, so that they felt guilty enough to go to early mass that morning to pray for the living or the dead, and having persuaded the telephone operator to make a special effort with the numbers because of the emergency, Cecile felt when her sister arrived that she had someone with whom to share her anxieties which were mounting as the sun rose over the plain and the central hills, where she could see the white egrets from the swamp curl like pink petals against the sunrise. They always gave her a sense of hope, but this morning she paid that hope little attention.

Father Sebastian came at once. He had asked the assistant priest to say the six o'clock mass and to say it for the repose of the soul of Philip Monagas who was about to die. It occurred to Father Sebastian that the prayers for Philip's soul might be said at the exact moment it was leaving his body. It would be a felicitous coincidence.

Cecile thought that Father Sebastian had come out of the room to request someone to answer the responses to the liturgy of the dying, but instead her earlier feelings of impropriety were compounded when he asked for two beers. In her shock Cecile got Alicia, the old nurse, to open the bottles and bring them up with mugs in order that the gentlemen might have the option not to drink from the neck of the bottle.

'My dear, they are now both drinking beer in the bedroom. I hate to think of communion sandwiched between beers.' Cecile held her sister's hand for strength.

'We've always said that we shouldn't drink before the sun has set, but they are taking it a bit too far, slipping them in before the sun has risen.' The sisters had to smile.

'Philip – he was always different.'

'The will?'

'The will? Well, it's all in the box under his bed with everything else we imagine to be there: the invention.'

Father Sebastian came out of the room carrying the strong-box. 'It won't be long now, my dears. You can go in and start the rosary. He is sleeping now and will eventually fade away. Angels will cradle him to paradise.'

While the sisters recited the rosary, kneeling at the bedside of Philip Monagas, his nieces were turning in their dreams of love. His brother came in and paid his respects and then returned to inspecting his stamps and watering his orchids. That morning the tide was out in the gulf and the sun was beginning to bake the mudflats which cracked, and a pelican perched on the rib-cage of a rotting hull of an old barnacled boat while herons pecked inquisitively, leaving their imprints on the remaining soft patches of sand. On the exposed seabed beneath the gnarled mangrove, crabs scuttled, clicking in the shadow of oysters, writing their hieroglyphs on the tablets of mud, telling a story to be tugged away at the next tide by the moon.

In his presbytery, sitting on the edge of his iron bed, Father Sebastian re-read the contents of Philip Monagas' last will and testament, having discovered in a brown envelope in the strong-box a letter appointing him his executor. In the gru-gru tree outside the window he heard the question of the keskidee, 'Qu'est-ce qu'il dit?' So he began to read aloud the wishes that the brand new typewriter and unblemished quarto of typing paper be given to the young stenographers above Miss Redhead's parlour; his pens, pencils, sharpeners and erasers to Miss Thomas's son with an avuncular note of advice to beware of professionals and be true to himself. There was a postcript, 'I found that going away from the island led to a tremendous need to return, but on returning I found that history had chained my words. I am sure you will do differently, eventually.' To Father Sebastian he left a single sheet of typing paper with four words written at the top; assumed to be the title of a story, maybe his life's work: 'A Very Sad Story'.

The Pond

There was this pond in the village
and little boys, he heard till he was sick
were not allowed too near . . .

. . . drawn hard by prohibitions

. . . he found himself
there at the fabled edge.

. . . shimmering in guilt,
he saw his own face peering from the pool.

from 'The Pond' – MERVYN MORRIS

Jonathan stood alone, shading himself under a flamboyant tree from the hot afternoon sun. This was the *last* day. BOYS' SCHOOL was over. The Christmas holidays had begun. He stood apart, waiting for the company school bus to arrive.

His friends who lived in San Andres were walking away down the promenade. Jai, Espinet, 'Reds', and Thorpe waved as they turned the corner into Penitence Street.

Jonathan thought he might not see them till after the Christmas holidays when they would all meet up at 'Pres'. Presentation College. He might see them downtown, Christmas shopping. They were bound to tease him when they saw him with his mother. He felt he wanted to invite them home. He remembered a story his mother once told him about his uncle when *he* had been at school. He had wanted to bring his school 'pardners' home for afternoon tea. When they came, they were black.

73

The story was always left like that.

The Sugarcane Company School Bus had arrived. The white college boys were getting in, shoving for the best seats, hanging out of the window with the usual chants, *Blackie cockroach, blackie cockroach.* Black boys standing in the dust under the shade trees, responded with their chants, *Whitey cockroach, whitey cockroach.*

The convent girls got in afterwards. The attention of the college boys in the bus turned to them. They stared at their white bodices, smooth over their small breasts. Their blue pleated skirts jumped as they moved down the aisle of the bus between the boys. The girls were bending over to peer out of the windows to wave to black friends outside. The college boys sniggered and jostled with each other.

Jonathan stared out of the window and noticed the black girls walking away. He noticed their white socks on their brown legs. He noticed their oiled hair, parted neatly. Their faces were shining, laughing, as they turned and waved to their friends in the bus.

Girls were different from boys.

The boys in the bus started up other chants, *Coolie, coolie come for roti, half past two,* as a group of Indian boys went by. They banged the sides of the bus, jumping up and slapping the glass windows and making monkey faces, *Whitey cockroach!*

The bus started up and then drove down past the promenade, leaving BOYS' SCHOOL, the convent and the town behind.

This was one world. This was the world Jonathan came to in the early morning, before the mists had lifted off the canefields. They had come through the villages with the dew still on the grass. Gangs of men and women were going out to the fields. Crop time in a month.

He entered the town before the shops had opened up, and already people were leaving who had been to the early market in Mucurapo Street.

Everyone got mixed up here. Then, in the afternoon, pushed out to their separate worlds.

The afternoon sun was behind them. They left the town, clustered haphazardly about the big hill in the centre, a landmark on the gulf coast. They passed through the villages full of afternoon life, children by the standpipes, men hanging out under the rum shops, women carrying shopping.

Then, the canefields. Canefields as far as the eye could see. They swayed in the breeze. Dust whipping up on the gravel traces. Haze and blur, as Jonathan leant out of the window of the bus with the breeze in his face, water in his eyes.

In the distance the tall palmistes. White columns against the blue. Plumes in the wind. Royal Palms.

These were the sugar estates. Another world. A white house stood on a hill, encircled by black galvanised barrack-rooms below in the gully.

Jonathan thought of the convent girls with their white socks on their brown legs, tight bodices over small breasts.

When he was smaller, he remembered playing with Gina and Betty. Dolly house. They were Mr Thomas's daughters. Mr Thomas was the barman at the company club, and lived behind the bamboo patch. Jonathan remembered that time, their smells, the food Mrs Thomas cooked. Moko, *pong* plantain. He remembered the pretty things in the little drawing-room. The silence when they crept into Mr and Mrs Thomas's bedroom, and saw themselves in the mirror.

But *they* did not come to play in *his* house.

Jonathan was distracted from his reverie. There was a fight at the back of the bus. The usual fight. A creole boy with a limey boy. Everyone in the bus was taking sides. Blows began to fly between boys in other parts of the bus. The girls, grown up, ignored the boys.

Jonathan stayed out of it. He remembered once when he had been goaded by his bigger brother to hit this limey boy in his face. He remembered how it had felt, his fist on the other's jaw bone.

Jonathan was relieved when he got off the bus opposite the sugar factory.

As he crossed the busy main road, he heard the hooter going off.

75

The sound of the siren filled the air. It was time for the labourers to go home.

Jonathan noticed a gang of boys coming up the road from working in the fields. They were boys his age, barefooted and besmirched with dirt. They didn't get to go to secondary school as he was going to do after the holidays with Jai, Espinet and Thorpe. He did not want to meet up with them. They might call out things as he was on his own, so he slid down the muddy bank to the edge of the pond.

Jonathan was not allowed to play by the pond alone. It was dangerous. Forbidden. Boys from the barracks had drowned there, stuck in the grey slime of the mud. There were alligators in the deep or lying menacingly in the reeds.

He felt excited, afraid and guilty as he stood at the edge of the pond doing something he shouldn't do. The mixture of these feelings made him feel different. His body tingled.

The same gang of boys he had seen coming up the road, were now coming down to the edge of the pond, further round by the pump-house where the water was sucked into the big grey pipes to the factory coolers. They took off their clothes and took a running dive into the brown water.

Jonathan felt scared.

The laughter of the boys came over the reeds with the sound of their splashing. He could see them, their black naked bodies slipping and falling on the mud in the shallows.

Jonathan watched.

He stooped, not wanting to be seen. From where he crouched, he examined the frothy surf at the edge of the pond among the reeds. Through the reeds he could see the naked boys.

The frothy surf was where the frogs' eggs hatched. Already Jonathan could see the tadpoles wriggling, black heads with little tails. Minute frogs were leaping into the slime on the bank. He examined them, seeing at the same time, his own face, reflected in the dull water.

There was a hole in a hedge which grew down to the edge of the pond. On the other side was the garden belonging to the company clubhouse. Jonathan crawled through the hole into the garden. This was a short cut home, but he also liked to pass through the garden just for the fun of it. The garden was enclosed by high hibiscus hedges and a lot of it was under the shade of a large saman tree. He walked around collecting a small bunch of flowers for his mother, stopping to stare at a hummingbird hovering over the throat of a flower. He liked the garden. It was mysterious and he often played hide-and-seek here with his friends. But this afternoon he was alone.

He lay down on the grass and went over it again – that this was his last day at BOYS' SCHOOL. He thought again about Jai, Reds and Thorpe. He closed his eyes and he saw tadpoles wriggling in the muddy water. Eggs in the frothy surf. He daydreamed.

'Ei, whitey, white boy, what you doing?'

Jonathan did not hear immediately. He had drifted off.

'Ei whitey, what you doing, sleeping in the grass?' The shrill, whispering voices woke him.

Jonathan leapt up and spun round to see the group of Indian boys. They stood looking down at him lying on the grass. They were naked. For a moment he just stared at their black, naked, wet bodies. Then he sprang up and ran out of the garden into the clubhouse yard, the Indian boys running after him and laughing. When they got to the clubhouse yard they turned and ran back down to the pond, crawling through the hole in the hedge and diving into the water.

Jonathan sat on the steps of the clubhouse, dazed, his heart thumping.

In the distance, he heard the *pick pock, pick pock* of the tennis players on the red clay courts on the other side of the clubhouse. The rhythm soothed him.

He heard the jangle of the golf bags as the golfers went down under the almond trees to tee off, followed by their caddies from the barracks.

He had left his bunch of flowers for his mother lying on the grass, while running away from the naked boys.

In the centre of the clubhouse yard there were the scattered parts of a merry-go-round waiting to be erected. This was going to be the central attraction of the annual Christmas party for the white children of the company. Tomorrow morning, Jonathan was going to help his mother give out sweet drinks, buns and toys wrapped in red cellophane, to the Indian children from the barracks. That would be *their* Christmas. But by the afternoon, the merry-go-round would be erected for the annual Christmas party. Father Christmas would be coming in a red gown and hood. Of course, he did not believe any more, but the ritual still excited him. He and his friends liked to guess who was the overseer dressed up this year.

Jonathan got up from the steps where he had waited till he was sure the boys had gone off to the barracks. He walked among the brightly painted wooden horses lying on their sides on the ground. Their legs were fixed in strides and gallops. Their tails were flying behind. Black eyes stared out of blue, red and yellow faces, startled at the end of outstretched necks. He stroked the flanks and his hands slipped over the smooth brightly painted wood. He felt disappointed. He knew what a real horse felt like, when he rode with his father. A real horse felt warm and nervous under his legs. It twitched under his touch.

Beyond the circle of light in which the merry-go-round revolved, there were widening circles of darkness. The small children screamed as the motor went faster and faster. Anxious parents, standing on the perimeter, watched the elated and shocked faces of their children turning away from them, hurtling into the darkness.

The wooden horses which had lain immobile on the ground the day before, appeared capable of magic in the flicker of the coloured lights and speed. They kept to their course. They never went beyond the circle of light.

'Can I get up with you?' Jonathan had noticed her smiling at him earlier, but he had not allowed himself to respond. She was one of the convent girls, but dressed differently now, in her frilly, pink, party dress sticking out around her.

'Yea, all right.' He made room for her in front of him on the blue and white horse. This was forbidden. He hoped that the merry-go-round man would not notice before they set off. The girl clung to the horse's neck and Jonathan's arm and pulled herself up.

The merry-go-round juddered and then began to move. Slowly at first, then faster and faster.

In the wind, her hair stung his cheeks. They screamed at each other out of excitement. Then he put his arms around her waist. She clung to the neck of the horse.

Beyond them was a blur, light and darkness streaked with speed.

Faces faded away from the sides. They were a tight knot. Flying away, magically.

Jonathan stared out into the darkness beyond the circle of light. He was leaning over the girl now and he could see her eyelashes over her closed eyes. He too closed his eyes. Tadpoles were wriggling in the muddy water. Frogs were alive in the slime of the mud. His own face looked back at him from the water. Wet, naked, black boys were swimming out of the darkness towards him. They had the faces of Jai, Reds, and Thorpe. The girl's body was warm against his chest. He continued to hold her. He wanted to kiss her cheek, but then he didn't. The music came over the roar of the motor, and the screams of the small children. It was from the new Elvis Presley film *Love Me Tender*.

They were beginning to descend. The motor was slowing down. The voice of Elvis was smooth and deep.

The clubhouse yard began to take its usual shape. Behind the hibiscus hedge in the mysterious garden, Jonathan could see a row of Indian boys looking into the light from the darkness.

The merry-go-round trembled to a standstill. Jonathan and the girl lay quite still for a moment. Then the girl slipped off the horse, holding on to his arm. He held her hand. His palm was sweaty. He looked down at her. 'You, all right?'

'Yea, I liked that. Bye.' She turned with a smile.

'Your name?' Jonathan called.

But she had run off into the club where the teenagers were dancing to Rock-and-Roll. He wanted to go after her.

He got off the horse and stood with his back to the hedge behind which the mysterious garden was in darkness.

'Ei, whitey, give me a ride.' He heard the same shrill whisper from the afternoon before.

'Ei, whitey, go and bring me a sandwich.' Another voice, soon a chorus in his ear.

He stood still, choked and cramped.

Jonathan walked away with a sharp pain in his back. He climbed the clubhouse steps. The magic spell had been broken and he now understood what was beyond the circle of light.

Suddenly, there was a rush of small children from inside the clubhouse and they went screaming down through the garden, down to the edge of the pond. Jonathan stood alone while everyone else drifted down, away from him.

Out in the middle of the pond, bobbing up and down, was a large white papier-mâché swan erected on a small dinghy. It was hung with yellow cellophane lanterns. Santa Claus was sitting inside, being rowed to the shore.

Jonathan walked away from the party. He did not want to wait for the arrival of Santa Claus. He turned away from the clubhouse, the merry-go-round, the pond with the papier mâché swan, and walked out on to the golf course.

It got darker and darker, the further he went.

I Want to Follow My Friend

1

Mrs Wainwright kept an eye on the two boys. She held them within her orbit with the affectionate touch of a restraining hand, guiding their inhibited play, as they both leant out of the window of the school bus. She watched them and smiled, parting their hair with her fingers, musing on how quickly they had grown. The smaller boy was her son, Christopher, the other was his best friend, David.

David was coming to spend the Easter holidays with them.

'Christopher?' He tugged away from her, the breeze in his face. 'Christopher, darling, why do you want to go to school at Mount Saint Maur?' Christopher did not turn to answer.

He shouted his reply to the wind, 'I want to follow my friend.' He shouted across the canefields, swishing past, bringing the smell of burnt cane. His words were lost to his mother, but enjoyed by his companion.

The boys resisted her, not out of malice, but because of their instinct for play. They linked their arms around each others' shoulders, holding each other in their laughing eyes.

Eventually, when they were tired of leaning out of the bus, they rested back in their seats, their eyes watering from the wind in their faces. Mrs Wainwright dabbed them with her hankerchief. And still the boys pulled back, squirming in their seats to avoid her attention. They were like small calves, all arms and legs.

Then, quite suddenly, as if by a miracle, their energy subsided and she was able to catch their attention. 'Now, Christopher, I want you to tell me why you're so keen to go to Mount Saint Maur?'

Christopher, his mother's 'little bearer of Christ', as she liked to call him, looked up into his mother's face and repeated seriously, 'I want to follow my friend.'

Mrs Wainwright listened and stared, startled by the unusual seriousness of her young son.

'Yes, because I'm there,' David said.

'I see,' said Mrs Wainwright, accepting what seemed an understandable response, yet nevertheless pondering her son's tone of voice.

The bus put them down near the Chapel of The Holy Innocents.

'Sybil, have you seen the boys?' Mrs Wainwright called out to her cook the following day after lunch.

'No, madam, I think those boys in the fields playing.'

Indeed, from her bedroom window, Mrs Wainwright caught sight of Christopher and David disappearing from her sight, as they entered a field of young cane which was not to be burnt this year.

They would be safe, she thought. They would play and then be back at tea-time.

Christopher and David ran on, deeper and deeper into the field of young cane. They felt that they were lost. When they looked up, they saw only the vivid blue sky, open and high, and the sun beating down.

They had been playing all morning nearer the house, in the yard itself, and climbing trees just beyond the hedge. Their play evolved, each making their demands and feelings known, bargaining for power, now David had it, now Christopher.

A whole imaginary world had been constructed in the sand-bank on the side of the bungalow. Losing themselves in this world, the two boys drove their toy cars and played at what they saw adults do. The struggle for a balance of power could go wrong here. It brought tears. Anger arose, and the kicking in of these self-created worlds.

After lunch they returned to their sand-bank, but the game no longer held its allure. In the heat, they sat on a bench and threw stones, seeing who could throw the furthest. But soon they were bored with this as well.

Then, a kind of silence fell between them. Then they had

butterflies in their stomachs. They exchanged looks and brushed against one another, feeling the skin on their arms tingle with an excitement which was different from throwing stones, or playing with dinky cars, or even climbing to the top of the tamarind tree, hanging on for dear life in the high wind.

'Let's go to the canefields,' said Christopher.

'Yea, let's,' David answered almost at once, as if they had had the same idea at the very same moment.

The field sloped increasingly. Eventually, they found themselves at the bottom of a gully. They were now quite far away from the bungalow.

No one would find them here.

They stopped running and sat down on the loose earth in the furrows between the rows of young cane. The wind sang through the serrated sugar-cane grass. They each knew why they had come here. They did not talk. Without any suggestion from the other, each boy began to take off his clothes.

They were barefooted, and forgot about what Christopher's father said about catching giggers.

Then they wrestled a little, laughing and tugging at each other's pants until they both fell on the ground. They pulled off their merino jerseys and squirmed in the soft, grainy earth which stuck to their skin. Their small penises grew hard.

From further down the gully, a train clanged along the line.

It was as if they were blind and feeling without seeing, touching each others' 'totees', rubbing them in their hands, cupping the tight, small balls. Nothing happened, just this tingling feeling – a feeling to go on and on. But nothing happened. It felt as if something might, but it didn't. Finishing this game like their others, they began putting on their clothes again and tied their jerseys round their necks.

Out of the gully, they entered an orchard of fruit trees. They climbed, picked and sucked grapefruit, the juice dribbling down their chests.

When they got back to the bungalow, Mrs Wainwright said, 'Ah, there you are. Run along and have a shower.'

That Easter holiday ended and Christopher looked forward to their August holiday together before he joined David at Mount Saint Maur.

'You'll have to be up at the crack of dawn.' His father spoke with relish, remembering his school. 'A cold shower.'

Christopher smiled, trying to be brave. His mother ran her fingers through his hair soothingly.

'Sports, plenty of sports, young man,' his father continued. 'Make a man of you.'

'Give him the present,' his mother said.

Mr Wainwright went off and returned with a long parcel. As it was presented to Christopher, both his parents looked on eagerly for his reaction.

No sooner had Christopher unpacked the cricket bat than his father took it from him. 'Got to stay in your crease, and you have to watch for the ball as it leaves the bowler's hand.' Mr Wainwright knocked the bat gently on the tiles of the verandah. *Pock, pock*. 'So,' he said, looking like a batsman waiting for the ball. He kept tightening his grip on the handle of the bat and looking up again at the imaginary ball. He feigned a stroke, going out a little from the imagined crease to meet the imaginary cork ball. He then settled back into his crease again. He ran his hand along the smooth side of the bat. 'You have to keep this well oiled, my man. We'll have to get you some linseed oil.' He handed the bat to Christopher, holding it firmly in the middle with the handle towards his son. 'You have a try.'

Christopher's mind was filled with the terror of the imaginary cork ball. He had watched the Indian boys on the savannah. He had heard the hard knock of the leather on the wood. He had seen the ball speed through the grass to the boundary. He looked down at the bat. It felt heavy and awkward in his hand.

'Well, you'll have to learn fast, young man.'

He heard his father. Young man.

His mother smiled encouragingly, but looked a little disappointed that he had not entered into his father's game.

Christopher put the bat in the spare room.

The house became filled with reminders of Christopher's imminent departure for boarding school. The Singer sewing machine was forever humming in the spare room. The floor was covered with threads and scraps of khaki and grey uniforms.

Christopher had to stand, to be measured and then for fitting. Pants and shirts were made a little too big. 'He'll grow into them,' Mrs Wainwright said to Miss Sing, the seamstress.

Christopher heard his mother and father.

Make a man of you.

He'll grow into them.

At siesta, when his father had gone back to work, Christopher lay next to his mother on the big bed. He looked at her face. It was changing. When she had fallen asleep he tiptoed out of the room. At the door, he looked back at her. Her face looked sad. Then he thought what she might look like if she was dead. He did not want her to die. He did not want to go away. He did not want anything to change.

Christopher tiptoed downstairs to one of the servants' rooms which was used as a junk room. He closed the door behind him. The only light came through the cracks in the jalousies.

In the corner of the room, there was an old trunk with old clothes and old carnival costumes. Christopher took off his clothes. He rummaged around in the trunk for his favourite costume. It was made of muslin, hand painted. Yellow and black. A butterfly costume. It was encrusted with sequins and beads. He stood in the half light transformed by the costume. His body tingled.

This was his game.

Play was like a deep soft bed into which to climb. A warm pool in which to swim.

Then, at last, David arrived for the end of the August holidays.

They played their usual games, but then they crept into the junk room at siesta when the house was asleep.

They took off their clothes and dressed and undressed. Butterfly. Bat. Emperor. Red Devil. They changed and changed into funny hats and wire masks.

They played in the half dark with the cracks of light, piercing shafts laden with dust.

The rains were heavy. They played in the rain and in the canals at the bottom of the gully. They swam naked. Dried off in the rain.

Siesta. They had their twilight world, in from the blinding sun. It seemed that something would happen, but nothing did. It could go on and on.

On the last day of the holidays, Christopher and David went as usual to the junk room. The dressing-up trunk was not there. The room had been tidied up. The shutters were open. It was a dull room.

They soon found out why.

In the spare room, where all of Christopher's clothes and equipment for boarding school were accumulating, the boys found the trunk. It was empty. There were little sachets of mothballs and cuscus grass lying at the bottom. It stood on the floor empty. Waiting. Soon, Mrs Wainwright would be packing the school uniforms, towels, linen, blanket, cardigans and shoes. There was a new toothbrush and toothpaste, soap. They were all heaped up on the bed. All his shirts and pants, towels, and linen had a number, 59, sewn on with his name, Christopher Wainwright, in red.

The cricket bat with a tin of linseed oil and shiny red cork ball lay next to the clothes.

On the top shelf of the press the boys found their costumes neatly stacked away.

The boys stared.

Christopher heard his mother and father.

Make you a young man.

He'll grow into them.

3

Christopher watched his father's car from the portico of the school, round the bend, move along the avenue of casuarinas. He followed it with his eye until it became a dot.

He imagined his mother and father driving over the plains alone.

He continued to look out, long after their car had disappeared.

The horizon was different from here.

The first night he could not fall asleep. David was somewhere else in the dormitory. He was one year ahead. He didn't know the boy next to him. There was a dim nightlight outside Father Benedict's

86

room which would stay on all night. Next to his bed, the cricket bat leaned up against his locker. He touched it and smelt the linseed on his fingers.

As the first term continued, Christopher and David saw less and less of each other. At first they had held together, a new boy with his more experienced friend, then, without understanding what it was, some force was pulling them apart. David was chosen by other boys. He moved around in a gang. They weren't the boys Christopher liked. It was not safe to be on your own, or to be with a single friend. There were loyalties and rivalries.

Boys who did not take part were sissies.

'Sissy, sissy,' a boy called. Christopher's eyes burnt, but he would not show that he wanted to cry. His hurt was deep. His anger, furious. He did not know what it meant, this change, but it felt like they wanted him to disown something quite close and precious to him. Or, to give them something. He sensed what it might be.

Why did some boys belong to one gang and others to another? Why couldn't he belong to David's gang? Why couldn't he be alone with David?

Their games in the holidays were a secret. They had always been a kind of secret. But here, they were definitely not to be spoken about. In a way, what they did, was a secret from themselves.

They avoided each other when other boys were around.

One afternoon, Christopher straggled behind the other boys back from the refectory after tea. He stood near a bonfire outside the woodwork shop. He was absorbed, kicking bits of wood into the fire and watching the shavings curl into the flames. Then he heard crunching footsteps on the gravel path. He turned to look. It was an older boy.

Christopher continued to throw bits of wood on to the fire. He watched the resin bubbling off the bark in the heat. Then he felt the older boy right next to him. The boy spoke softly. 'I want to kiss you like if you were a girl.' Then he walked away.

Christopher turned to say something. What should he say? 'Wait.'

The boy was well ahead of him. He began running up the steep, stony path to the college.

'Wait,' Christopher shouted again, trying to catch up. Confused, but wanting to say something. 'Wait.' Christopher slipped on the gravel. The boy had lost him.

Christopher felt dejected. Something had stirred in him. He thought of how he had lost David. He turned back from where he had fallen and took the lower path into the forest behind the college. This was out of bounds, but he decided to risk it.

He felt like he used to feel when he was smaller and had climbed to the top of the tamarind tree. Dangerous. Quite quickly he was climbing into the hills, looking down on the college. He could see the other boys like little dots, running around. He kept from where other boys might be climbing themselves, finding secret places to smoke. He skirted the old scout's den with the list of measurements scratched forcibly into the wooden walls. *Timothy de Freitas has the biggest cock.*

Christopher found himself running now, slipping and grabbing hold of the young saplings. His heart was pounding in his chest. He had a stitch in his side. He was beginning to cry. His lips were trembling.

He reached a clearing where it was different from the shadows of the forest. The light was streaming down from the afternoon sky.

High in a blue sky, he saw a flock of green parrots. Then, suddenly, the air was full of their screams.

He was thirsty. He decided to head down to the valley where the river flowed over large rocks.

Suddenly, he saw it. His heart was in his mouth. A pink and black coral snake was entwined on a branch which lay across the track. He knelt down quietly and picked up a stone and a stick. He hit the branch with the stick and the snake slithered to the ground. But before it could slide away into the grass, Christopher threw his stone and then another and another, a large one falling on the snake. It was crushed.

Long after he knew that he must have killed it, Christopher continued to heap stones upon the snake, crushing its head. He was deliberate. He wanted it dead.

When he was finished he felt exhausted. He sat down and dried his eyes. Then he realised that all the while he had been crying.

Christopher found the river and drank from his cupped hands lying on his belly across a rock.

In the days which followed, Christopher still wanted to talk to the boy who had said that he wished to kiss him. He didn't get a chance.

He wrote him a letter, keeping it in his pocket. It burnt his leg with its presence.

Then he tore it into small pieces and threw it on the bonfire one afternoon, where he stood on the gravel path, straggling behind the other boys.

Waiting.

Sylvia's Room

It was an apartment in a broken-down part of the city. It was in an old part of the old town by the cemetery with the arch of blue stone.

From the back gallery, with the high ceiling and the awning painted green and white, Sylvia could see the burial places of the old families. She could see the vaults with their cupolas. There were the old monuments of the old white families and the free coloured. She recalled some of the names she had read walking through the cemetery on a Saturday afternoon with her mother when she was a little girl. *Metivère, Vessiny, Nivet* and *de Lapeyrouse* which gave its name to the old cemetery.

They christen. They marry. They bury. *Maingot* with *D'abadie*.

They were the same names on the woodlice-ridden old varnished pews at the front, by the communion rails of the old Catholic churches of the city. This was her mother's pilgrimage. *Sacred Heart, Saint Patrick's, Rosary*. The culmination of Saturday afternoon was the cathedral. *Immaculate Conception.*

Daily, daily sing to Mary . . .

That time smelt of incense and old prayer books.

But now, as she looked out from the gallery of her small apartment, she thought, it all change. Both the rich and the poor are buried there. All go now, into the same ground under the wall by the frangipani tree.

Sylvia had come back. She had gone away, left the island, and come back. The sepulchres, which had their own grandeur and stature when she had stood in front of them, were dwarfed by the tall trunks of the Royal Palms.

Charles Kingsley on his visit to the island in 1880 had remarked on

90

the palmiste, *tall, fanning into plumes; doric columns of ancient Greece*. She
read that in one of these new books put out by a local publisher. Sepia
photographs of old families. Family groups, weddings, christenings,
muslin and lace, a black shadow in the background. These were
accompanied by quotes from colonial writers. A last ditch attempt to
hold on to a faded past. *Folie de grandeur*. Antiquarian. She let her eyes
travel up the trunks of the palmiste to the tip-top extravagance of
their flowering. They were like the plumes on the top of the
governor's hat. *The governor tall tall tall he peeping over the wall* she
hummed the old time calypso.

The wind wrung the flowering extravagance. The trunks stood
unmoved.

On the ledge of the verandah there were pots with ferns and cactus.
Sylvia spent this afternoon like other afternoons, on her own. She
turned the soil in the little pot of cactus. She sprinkled some water
and pressed the earth at the centre. She liked these plants. Ferns,
cactus, and above all, her aloes.

'Sylvia, you watering your plants, child?' the Indian woman in the
apartment downstairs called up. Sylvia knew that she was telling her
again that the water was seeping down to her verandah from the
ferns.

'Is all right, Miss Naipaul. It go dry soon.'

That was the extent of their exchanges. Miss Naipaul drew her
knowledge from peeping through her jalousies and moving the edge
of her lace curtains when Sylvia went down to the street. It was never
her face that she saw, but the movement of the curtain, or a shadow
through the jalousie cracks.

Sylvia mixed herself a rum and took in her other view, the sea. It
was uncanny how the sea was higher than the land in this part of the
old town. You looked up to the ships when you were walking in the
street. From the verandah, she was on a level with the tankers out on
the gulf. Their masts were like giant needles, threaded. Further out,
more needles, needles of rain stitching the sky.

The gulf was known for its sudden squalls.

She had been frightened standing on the deck of the French liner next
to her sister Cecilia, waving to her family below. Her father had said

91

that it was good for them to go and stay by their Aunty Gertrude in London. They would get an education.

She had the names for London. Trafalgar Square. The Mall. Piccadilly Circus. Buckingham Palace. Pictures in a picture book.

There will be possibilities for the girls, her father argued with her mother, putting money aside each month from loading on the wharf.

It was just getting dark as they stood on the deck. Waving, being brave. A band was playing. That's how they did it then. Music. Streamers.

There was an orange sunset.

Sylvia and her sister stayed up on deck till they couldn't see the island any more. But, for a long while, they saw the beam from the Chacachacare lighthouse. Off, on. Off, on. Then they saw nothing.

The next morning was Barbados. And then, each day, another island, for five days, delaying her departure. Then on the sixth morning, there was only sea. Sea. She was sick. The tune from one of the French island bands continued in her head . . . *adieu foulard*. The pretty women waving their scarves.

Southampton. Mist. Gulls. A train. She had never felt so alone. Cut off.

Sylvia turned her back on the sea and the cemetery. She went inside.

The room had been arranged quite carefully. For a long while now, she had spent her evenings alone, arranging it and herself in it. Distinct characteristics of the original architecture had survived. She had wanted to keep the fretwork, like bands of lace between the top of the walls and the ceiling. The wood had rotted. The landlord, Miss Naipaul's brother, had replaced it with breeze blocks with diamond-shaped holes for ventilation. Sylvia avoided looking at them. Subdued lights under plaited palm shades made the ceiling disappear in the evening when she used the room.

She missed the lacy shadows in the early morning sunlight thrown upon the mosquito net and walls of her bedroom when she was a child.

She knew she was trying to recreate her room in that little Belmont house where she had lived before she went away. She would lie there, waiting to be told to get up for school. The ceiling and walls were freckled with moving shadows.

Her mother had left the house much earlier in the pitch dark, having to get to the Monagas house the other side of The Savannah in St Clair. She brought back stories of the Monagas children, getting them up for school, giving them their breakfasts. Marie-Claire and Andresito. She talked about them like they were her own children. Sylvia could still remember the names.

The Monagas name was in the cemetery, under the statue of an angel with a broken arm. She remembered her mother pointing it out. That is where the madam people bury.

Where were her ancestors buried?

The wooden floors were still there. Varnished now, not scrubbed white pitch pine. Floors used to be scrubbed in the big houses on the The Savannah by Indian women from Aranguez. They scrubbed and their bracelets jangled. She saw them once, peeping through the pantry door in the Monagas house when she accompanied her mother one day instead of going to school.

Sylvia continued her painting. She was painting over the old dirty colonial cream. Paint too expensive, Mr Naipaul had said, wash it down, it go look good, you go see.

She knew there was another instinct at work. There was the high-ceilinged room in a Georgian terrace in Chelsea. There were white walls with net curtains to exclude the voyeur, give a view from the interior. This was where she had ended up, though she hadn't had much of an education.

She had style, he had said. *Black is beautiful*. He taught her taste. Big contracts. She had bone structure. She was his model. She lived in the whirl of Chelsea. *Chelsea Girl*.

He pimped her. Yes, that's what she felt now. Gave her a son.

To survive, she had to kill half herself. Leave her child. Get out. Come back.

Sylvia woke suddenly. It was the heat. Not a breath of air. She had nodded off taking a rest from her painting. Someone was knocking. Miss Naipual, she was knocking on her ceiling. There was a methodical two knocks, a pause, two knocks. Then she heard her behind the apartments under the gallery. 'Sylvia, Sylvia, you there, girl?'

At first Sylvia thought she wouldn't answer. Let her call, the noisy bitch. What could it be? Miss Naipaul was usually asleep by this time.

'Yes, Miss Naipaul, what is it?'

'Telephone, girl, come quick, is London, London calling.'

Sylvia then remembered that she had arranged with Miss Naipaul, in case of emergency, to take calls for her. Here it was, Miss Naipaul would know all her business. TELCO had still not installed her phone. But this was the first time anyone had called. *London calling*. It must be Toby. His father had wanted him called that. Everyone was calling their son Toby, at the time.

'Coming, Miss Naipaul.' Sylvia went down the back stairs.

'Child, is London, imagine that, they speaking like they next door.'

'Hello, hello.' The line was terrible. Crackling, and echoes giving back what she was saying, so that she had to pause to hear her own greeting and then hopefully hear who was calling her. 'Hello, dammit, man.'

'Girl, speak properly, is London, London calling.' Miss Naipaul, dressed for bed, was hovering.

'Yes, Toby, is that you sweetheart?'

'Who? Roland? Why are you calling me? How did you get this number?

'I see. Toby. What is it? Is something wrong? Is Toby OK?'

'You're sending him out? When? Let me speak to him?'

'Toby? Is that you? Are you OK sweetheart, darling? Are you OK?

'Of course I want you. Of course I love you. Yes, I have a place. I have a home. I have a job.

'What's that bastard saying? Roland?'

'Speak properly, girl, is London calling.'

'Fuck, the line has gone. Miss Naipaul, shut up. I'm sorry. It's my boy. He's coming. They'll call again. Miss Naipaul you must call me at once. I'm sorry.'

'Child, you have some language, you so quiet like a mouse upstairs, going in and out like is a mystery, but you have some language. You not learn that in England. I bet is right here so, you learn that since you come back.'

94

'Miss Naipaul, call me. I upstairs.'

It was all so sudden.

Sylvia poured herself another rum.

She looked about her. She was making a place for herself. Yes. She felt some relief at the way she had put the pieces together. There was a square of straw-coloured rush matting in the middle of the floor. Cheap. She thought. Only forty dollars in the Chiney shop in Charlotte Street. The Chinaman had told her it came direct from China. There was a cushion at her feet. She imagined someone curling there. Casual. The cushion was covered with a cotton print, a silkscreeen pattern, bamboo clump, green and brown.

She had a nice place. She sipped her rum.

More cushions with tasteful prints were scattered around the room. They were arranged to look scattered.

Apparent disorder.

Toby. She said his name.

She took in each piece. An interior decorating mind. She kept arranging and rearranging. Two coffee tables, magazines on one. On the other, some pottery. Concealed lighting. She had started some pottery herself. She needed to make that pot. The blue piece. Blue with an oxide stain where the glaze can bubble in the kiln. She must make that piece.

Toby.

She had a third rum.

She moved to the straight-back chair. Wooden slats hung with canvas. Behind it a standing lamp with a basket shade. Made by the Society for the Blind. They did good work. As she moved, she knocked a collection of calabash which rocked and rattled full of beads.

Oh, Toby.

She picked up some photographs which had fallen out of an old album on to the floor. She picked out a family group. Her father is wearing a brown suit and hat. Her mother is in a long white dress with a Victorian collar. Embalmed, she thought. They were fixed against a backdrop of Windsor Castle and incongruously, a single palm stood on a wooden pedestal in Wong's Studio in Belmont. She remember their hopes for her. There her mother and father stood, framed against what they thought were their dreams.

Sylvia put the album down and walked out on to the back verandah.

It was night. Amber. Phosphorescent. Smells from the China Palace and perfume from the frangipani under the wall, mixed with the jangle of traffic. The city was alive. She wanted to go out.

She couldn't see the sea or the cemetery.

'Sylvia!' A hard knock and then her name again, 'Sylvia, is your boy! Come quick!'

Afterwards, when she had climbed the back stairs, she paused by the ledge with the aloes. She picked up the small pot and pressed the earth.

Aloes.

Yes. Come.

Come, son.

The House of Funerals

1

The morning sun blazed down hot on to the small, rusty-roofed houses with filigreed, white, lattice-work verandahs, yellowing. Fern baskets, hanging from eaves festooned with cobwebs, dripped.

The tumble-down town tumbled down to the wharf in the bay on the gulf and jangled with Indian music. On the High Street loudspeakers blared from the doorways of Ramnarine's Garment Palace and shattered the glass cases in Patel's Jewel Box.

The sea in the bay on the gulf glinted.

Above the traffic and the commerce of the town, on top of the hill with the fir trees, the jangle achieved a monotony. The heat, like a mirage, floated above the pitch road cut into the ochre earth winding up the hill.

On the gulf the mirage hung above the glinting, clamped downfast, leaden lid of the sea; the grey lid of an ancestral vault.

The jangling tumbled-down town, the sweating morning, the jalousies-shuttered room behind Teresa's Hairdressing Salon to which Gaston, the grandson of Cecile Monagas went 'to play in the dirty water with that coolie girl' as his mother would say, the grave-diggers in Paradise Cemetery, the women in the flower shop entwining sweet-lime bushes into wreaths with tuberoses and cata-lair orchids, the women of the Legion of Mary and Father Sebastian the parish priest, all waited expectantly for the news that Cecile Monagas de los Macajuelos had eventually died.

2

Now on top of the hill in the garden with the fir trees there was the house: a vantage point from which to see the plains seeping from the swamps towards the continental cordillera of mountains in the north; the cocoa hills, ridged and green like the back of an iguana, rising and falling across the centre of the island; the dusty fringes of sugar cane disappearing into the southern forests, black with oil – the blue-stone house in the garden with the fir trees overlooking the gulf; each blue-stone quarried from the cliffs near the sea on the north coast of the island and brought to the top of the hill by African men, women and children: overseered, cajoled and sometimes paid weekly by Carlos Monagas de los Macajuelos; watched by Madoo the nightwatchman, the son of an indentured labourer, so that the people in the shacks below the hill would not steal the bricks and iron rods for the foundations in order to build their own fragile huts in the shadow of the blue-stone house; in the shadow and the shade of its courtyards, terraces, staircases leading to sunken gardens of roses and anthurium lilies growing beneath mango trees – the house with the grotto of the Blessed Virgin Mary at the end of the path near the calabash tree whose interior was cool with ferns potted in damp black earth and palms growing beneath arches and under alcoves in whose recesses there were busts of Venus and other goddesses: floors of polished parquet, mahogany chairs, tables, marble-topped chests of drawers from the sale of Napoleon the Third's palace, crystals and china in cabinets, portraits on the walls. In the bedroom of the house above the orchid house at whose windowsill she used to stand and watch the gulf and pray to the Virgin, Cecile Monagas de los Macajeulos died at dawn. She had been dying for years.

'Poor dear. Mariana my child this is the end of an era.' Marie-Claire, the sister of Cecile, stroked the hair of her niece. They touched their eyes with embroidered, linen handkerchiefs, blotting the first tears.

The purple, pink, white and gold blooms which perched like carnival butterflies upon the rubbery leaves growing out of the dry logs encrusted with dry moss, hung from wires in the orchid house, rotting.

Carlos Monagas, Cecile's husband, had grown them and then died from inhaling nicotine and the fungal dust.

Carlos had died at Pentecost and the church had to be stripped of its festive red and draped in black for the requiem. The vases of red exhoras were banked in the sacristy.

He was buried in the ancestral grave beneath the marble angel with the broken arm. Someone had wanted to steal the bouquet of lilies from the clenched fist of the messenger of heaven.

Cecile then began to die. Carlos her rock of Gibraltar had sunk into the gulf or that is what her sister and family thought. 'This will be the end of Cecile.' What they saw sitting near to the casket like one of Carlos's orchids, white and wearing a purple dress, was a stunned Cecile. Like a butterfly which, buffeted and knocked suddenly to the ground, as suddenly takes to the air for a day, to freedom: Cecile's freedom was like that of the butterfly.

She bought a car and could be seen at all parts of the island recording the changing landscapes of both the dry and wet seasons; holding on for dear life to her easel as she faced the windswept ocean raging in from off the Atlantic, so that she could depict the last detail in the yellowing frond of a coconut tree, bent to the brink of the water with its crown twisted back towards the land by the force of the wind. She became daring and swore at the sky which resisted being captured in a drop of coloured water on her white pad. 'They change so quickly,' she used to say, stamping her feet. She could be found in remote country villages painting the shacks of the poor and village women with baskets on their heads.

Her enthusiasm for life was so intense after the death of Carlos that she would come home quite amazed at the happiness of the world. 'Why was everyone smiling and waving at me today on the way back from Mass? The town was so happy as I was going down High Street.'

'But Mummy, you're mad. High Street is a one-way street, an up street.'

'Don't tell me that dear. It could only be Saint Christopher and the hosts of guardian angels who saved me.'

She broke through traffic lights in her eagerness.

But this burst and last claim on life was as short-lived as the life of a butterfly because the pain and endurance of the years had already destroyed her nervous system. Her last paintings became abstract as she could no longer control her fingers. They were splodges, blotches; the bursting of atoms, molecules, elemental. The water and the paints on the windowsill dried up. The last entries in her diary were dots, waiting, trying to steady her fingers.

The tinkle of the viaticum alerted Marie-Claire and Mariana as Father Sebastian entered the house of funerals followed by the acolyte with the bell and the bucket of holy water. Alicia the old nurse followed behind.

The women worked fast fearing putrefaction. They washed the thin, dead limbs of Cecile's body with soap and water. She was dressed in a blue nightgown because blue is the colour of Our Lady. Marie-Claire shook her head remembering, 'Mariana, I can see her now.'

'Aunty don't start remembering. I don't want to know.'

Marie-Claire sprinkled eau-de-Cologne on to a linen handkerchief and dabbed the forehead of Cecile's body. Afterwards she put the handkerchief to her nose and shook her head. 'I can see her now. I can see her as a bride.'

'Mr Samaroo is coming for the body, Aunty, and Father Sebastian is here.'

'Yes, dear. She died before she could receive communion, but now she is in His arms,' she whispered while stroking the limp hair on Cecile's head.

The women knelt and received the viaticum intended for Cecile. Father Sebastian broke the host into four parts with a crumb for the acolyte. 'This will help you on your way,' he chuckled. He anointed the body of Cecile Monagas de los Macajuelos with the extreme unction: her forehead, lips, ears, nose, eyes, and he stroked the fingertips and the extremity of the toes.

'Mr Samaroo, take care,' Mariana helped to lift her mother's corpse. 'Don't let me down.'

'Madam?' Samaroo's had been preparing bodies for burial in San Andres since before the beginning of the century.

'I'm coming for Mummy at two-thirty. The funeral in the church is at four o'clock.'

'Plenty time Madam.'

'The funeral in the church is at four o'clock and I don't want anything to interfere with that. You know how many funerals they have in this town.'

'Take care going down the steps,' said Mr Samaroo the professional.

'At twelve o'clock the women of the Legion of Mary will come and say the rosary and keep vigil. Then there is clothes. Aunty what I going to dress Mummy in now?' Mariana's voice cracked.

'We will think of something dear,' Marie-Claire followed behind the little procession down the stairs: Mr Samaroo and his attendant carrying the body helped by Mariana, Father Sebastian, the acolyte and Alicia. From the bay window of the staircase Marie-Claire could see the gulf.

The sea was like a slate in the vanishing dawn. 'So, Mr Samaroo, have your business finish on time.'

'Yes, Madam. You want the body to leave the home at three-thirty?'

'She has to leave from here. This is where she lived. This is where her children born and died. She buried them from here, though she believed that they had flown like angels across the gulf.' Mariana's voice trailed off.

'Yes, Madam. I see what you mean.'

'Do you? That is more than I can see. But you understand. She is not going to fly out over the gulf; assumed into heaven body and soul this afternoon. So please do your business properly this morning. You see this heat. Take care the body smell.'

'Madam you know how we does do business. Since my great-grandfather doing this thing. OK boy, rest down here, open the hearse door.'

'Take care, she so frail,' Alicia keened.

All the time Marie-Claire muttered, 'May the angels of heaven take her in their arms to Paradise.'

'And the advertisement, Madam, since 1888 we working for people in distress and now we have these new methods from America.'

'All the same Mr Samaroo heat is heat.' When she was a little girl her grandmother said that she looked as delicate and pretty as a porcelain figurine on the dressing-table of Marie Antoinette. She had grown old giving birth to sons.

The procession dispersed; Mr Samaroo with the corpse and Father Sebastian's blessing.

'Father Sebastian, the bells, you won't forget to toll the bells?' Mariana cried out to the priest.

'Quite right Mariana. Good of you to remember the bells.' Marie-Claire turned to go into the house.

Alicia, who was reputed to be a hundred years old, returned to the servants' quarters with her ancestry. Her father had been an English overseer and her mother an African slave. She came from Barbados to be nurse to generations of Monagas children. In the courtyard outside her room she looked up to the sky, 'Miss Mariana, Miss Mariana, corbeaux circling in the sky.'

At that moment a fast car with screeching tyres drove up into the yard; skidding on the pods from the flamboyant tree. 'Oh god all yuh, get out me way nuh.' It was Gaston, Mariana's son.

'Where have you been all night? In that dirty water again?' Mariana turned to go into the house.

This was Gaston, grandson of Gaston Monagas de los Macajuelos, great-grandson of Gaston Monagas de los Macajuelos from the matrilineal blood; the descendant of caballeros and conquistadors with fat features and dark shadows over his eyes. His shirt was open and gold chains with medals of Our Lady of the Immaculate Conception and Saint Christopher nestled in the hairs of his chest. He was sweating. 'God all yuh, leave a man alone nuh. Give a man a chance nuh.'

'Your grandmother died in the night and that is where you spend the night, shaming me and your father and the name of your family,' Mariana screamed.

'My father, shame?'

'Madam, son.' Alicia raised her eyes to the sky searching the circling corbeaux.

The bedroom above the orchid house overlooking the gulf was left to air. The bedspreads were pulled off and the mosquito net drawn back. Cecile had died on her marriage bed. It was made of saman wood, cut from a tree in the pasture of her father and grandfather's estate. The carpenter had built, under the instructions and design of her husband, a canopy giving her the shade which is given beneath those trees. It rose to a crown carved with wild English flowers from which hung the capacious folds of the fine mosquito net, like the train of her daughter-brides, or her own bridal lace, or that of her mother and grandmother before her.

It was a bed of births and deaths into which had soaked the amniotic waters, the blood of the womb and the vaginal tissue. It was the bed into which she had miscarried nine times: baptising with water from the basin near her bed; with her own hands and prayers; in hope and faith the soul had already filtered like sunlight through muslin or a blue afternoon. She dipped her fingers into the salt of the amniotic water and searched for tongues, ears, noses, fingers, and toes to anoint.

'Do you renounce Satan and all his works?' she asked and immediately whispered back to herself, 'I do.' She whispered again, 'And all his pomp?' Again, 'I do.' She spoke for the formless and speechless lips, wet between her legs, or which she pulled up to her breasts to suckle in hope; umbilically tied so that she was even more entitled to speak for them.

The little white satin-covered coffins which were lined with quilted taffeta were brought to this bedroom nine times for those rescued from limbo by the ministrations of Cecile Monagas de los Macajuelos.

Bells in the parish church of San Andres rang with joy nine times for the little angels assumed into heaven.

Marie-Claire pulled off the linen sheets; damp with the sweat of death. She looked at the bed and shook her head. They had all known and kept silent.

She remembered the convent girl in the dormitory hidden beneath the linen shroud to change her clothes; hiding from her own body, a child of nuns with crisp habits and linen veils.

They had all been so excited. 'We are going to give out Cecile's engagement,' her mother had announced on the verandah. She could see her now in the armchair near the ledge with the angel-hair ferns. She filled the chair with her broad hips sitting with her snow-white hair, the mending basket at her feet and the low mahogany table set with cups and saucers for tea. 'Carlos Monagas has been to see your father.' The old French family to be united with the old Spanish family; there was great excitement.

The grave of his ancestors was in the ancient city of San José de Orunya, where the river has run dry and the spirits float in the candlelit air on All Souls night.

Mrs de Lapeyrouse had dug deep into her chest for the old, soft lace of her own wedding dress. There was no time to wait for a dress from Paris. Carlos was leaving for South America. The wedding day would be within the month. Cecile wore gold on her wedding day. The lace had turned yellow; penetrated by moths.

Marie-Claire dusted the room. She paused at the window-ledge and stared out over the gulf. The images of her sister's girlhood rose to meet her from the leaden vault.

She had been so frail, so pale; like the white of blanched almonds in her yellowing dress. Carlos had thought of her as an orchid; like the orchid that he had found near the bleached drift wood at Galeota.

Then the morning at the wharf when they all waited to say farewell and to board the old rusting steamer, *La Concepcion*. Marie-Claire remembered turning to her mother, 'Mother, what will she do? What does she know?'

'Carlos Monagas is a gentleman,' her mother smiled, remembering her own wedding night at sixteen.

When Cecile returned from South America it was left to Father Sebastian to guide her soul and to bury the dead angels.

3

The afternoon stretched out into the eternity which Father Sebastian had prayed for. The traffic jam began to build up in the High Street. Gaston, Mariana's son, parked his fast car in the open gutter. He went into the back room at Teresa's Hairdressing Salon. As his mother would say, and Alicia deplore, 'to play in the dirty water', but his father, thumping him on the shoulder, would advise him, 'Take care with them young Indian beti, boy.' The loudspeakers proclaimed their bargains. The Indian music sang high in the telephone and electric wires strung out low over the emblazoned roofs. Zinc creaked and syncopated rhythms throbbed from taxis and transistors.

104

The verandahs dripped.

The sea crinkled like galvanised roofs into the blue afternoon which stretched like membrane over the skeleton of a mountain in Venezuela.

The time of Cecile Monagas lived on. It lived on in the linen sheets; washed in suds and sunned in the courtyard; shaken and ironed by Alicia; folded and brought up on a wooden tray for her madam to count and arrange in the linen press on the landing at the top of the steps in the blue-stone house. Cecile Monagas's time lived on: her fingers lived on in the embroidery on the pillowcases; in the tablecloths bargained for on the front steps of the blue-stone house with the Syrian merchant who brought his suitcases from Lebanon; in the filigreed lace which ran through the brown fingers of Mr Khan from Madras; in the doily mats from Madeira brought by the Portuguese wholesaler who had climbed Mount Mora in the hot sun.

Cecile Monagas had lived her time. It was accounted for in the shopping lists recorded at the back of her diaries, each item costed; in the weekly checks of the linen to see that the servants had not been stealing; in the lists of the babies' layettes; nine layettes kept in tissue-paper and preserved in moth-balls, but sweetened with cuscus grass from Dominica. There were christening gowns which had never been worn, lace bonnets and skull caps. Her presence lingered on in the souvenirs of her honeymoon and other paraphernalia of a young bride.

Her time was in the arrangements of flowers which young brides remembered in the sanctuary on their wedding day and which startled first communicants by the perfume of the frangipani bouquets. These were the same first communicants who were instructed in their faith and remembered her like a second mother. She gave them, at seven years old, a profound initiation into the mysteries of the immortality of the soul; why Adam and Eve were banished from the garden of Eden by an angel with a flaming sword and why Eve would bring forth children in sorrow and pain; of mortal sin and how far venial sin stretched; of efficacious grace; the infallibility of the Pope; the transubstantiation of bread into flesh and wine into blood; the ascension of the Lord; His transfiguration and the assumption of His mother, the Virgin, into heaven, complete with

105

body and soul. These truths, like the eternity of the afternoon; these words, possessed the time of Cecile Monagas; so intimately were they part of her that they kept recurring on the lips of the old women of the Legion of Mary that morning in the sacristy while they polished the brass candlesticks which would stand on either side of the black, draped catafalque on which the coffin of Cecile Monagas would rest at the centre of the church.

Ever since early morning, when he had anointed the body of Cecile Monagas, Father Sebastian had been remembering her confessions. He alone possessed a part of her which had now floated above the gulf into the clear dawn of the distant mountains of Venezuela; her invisible soul.

He remembered her, early, before the six o'clock mass, in the line for the confessional.

'Bless me, Father, for I have sinned, Father it is one day since my last confession.'

At first, he used to be surprised when he slid back the varnished, latticed shutters, to hear the small voice of Cecile Monagas yet again, when she had only been there the morning before. But then he became accustomed to her almost daily visits to him, as the representative of her God, the judge and forgiver of her sins.

'My child there is no need for you to come each day.' The priest felt that he had no other alternative but to try and restrain her need to come to him each morning; particularly when Cecile could not formulate precisely the name of her sin and its dimensions, but only that she carried about within her a sense of the enormity of sin and that she was sinful by nature.

'My child, for your penance I want you to say your daily rosary with special devotion for those souls who are trapped in purgatory and for the sins of the world, which weigh down upon the shoulders of our crucified Lord and which pierce the heart of His Virgin Mother.' He knew that these intentions would give her enormous joy and purpose.

It took Cecile years to come to a formulation of her sin. At first she thought that there were so many. Like the story of the gospel: 'My name is Legion for I am many.' She imagined her sin like little devils pricking into her with their tridents, like the *jab molasse* at carnival or the devils in the murals on the walls of the convent. They were

106

scruples which interrupted her daily activities: that she hadn't kissed her husband's cheek with sufficient fervour before he went to work; she had not completed her mending; or that a crumb had passed her lips inadvertently before going to the six o'clock mass and she had received communion having broken her fast; she had lost her temper with Alicia; she felt too exhausted to play with the children; she had not weeded the rose-bed with Madoo and the bajac ants had invaded on floating leaves upon the water in the anti-formica clay pots and stripped leaves and petals from Our Lady's roses. They arrayed themselves and invaded with such persistence. She had made a noise and disturbed Carlos in the stillness of the orchid house as she crushed the pebbles so they crunched and he was rustled from his velvet scents, nicotine and the fungal dust.

Her visits to Father Sebastian became more frequent. She needed to see him before and after mass. She visited him in his office in the presbytery, because during mass, at the crucial moment of the consecration she was filled with a sense of sin; she remembered seeing her body in the mirror of the bathroom and so she was unworthy to receive the host.

Father Sebastian had to become more than just her parish priest and confessor. He became her spiritual director.

She gave him her soul: the most secret and immortal part of herself; into his hands, soft with blue veins; smelling of hosts, holy oils and incense. His breath always had a stale, sweet smell of the communion wine, the blood of Christ. She gave to him that part of herself she taught the children to take most care of in order to direct heavenwards away from the pit of hell and its scrupulous devils.

At lunchtime the women of the Legion of Mary went to Samaroo's to keep the afternoon vigil and to say the rosary. They arrived as the attendants wheeled out from the embalming room the prepared body of Cecile in its mahogany casket with simple brass handles and cross upon the lid. She was arranged in quilted satin like an artificial orchid in a plastic box you give loved ones on birthdays and anniversaries. Mariana and Marie-Claire had sent her purple lace dress. Mr Samaroo, with the power of all his art, skills and new methods from America, had arranged what little hair was left into a nimbus of silver curls.

In the presbytery Father Sebastian sat alone at the lunch table gathering the crumbs of bread into little mountains. The fan on top of the corner cupboard whirred and swivelled, giving him an intermittent breeze. The water jug sweated dripping into the tablecloth. He squashed a soft grain of rice between his fingers. That morning he had thought of crushed wheat and stamped grapes at the consecration.

In the orchid house below the bedroom of the blue-stone house the orchids on their logs were still rotting. The birds which were accustomed to sing and flick silver from the bird bath in their flight, had vanished into the sizzling stillness. The pipe in the orchid house dripped, filling the barrel so that it eventually overflowed, and the water seeped through the pebbles to the underlying moss, all the time saturating the stone walls, growing with ferns, oozing into the beds with anthurium lilies, like a wet grave.

While the housekeeper did the washing-up Father Sebastian hung up his cassock behind the door of his bedroom and lay down in his vest and underpants beneath the whir of the ceiling fan. The Indian music from the bargain parade continued to advertise the seventy-five-per-cent discount in honour of the day, the coming weekend, the next weekend, the recession and the inflation. The picture of the Sacred Heart knocked against the wall in the hot air.

Gaston's car was still parked in the gutter with the dirty water running down the drain. He was still in the back room of Teresa's Hairdressing Salon.

The back room of Teresa's Hairdressing Salon kept its shutters closed so that the room sweated and the bedsprings creaked endlessly into the afternoon under the weight of Gaston's oppression. The weight of centuries humped into that ridiculous bottom. He had forgotten that it was the day that his grandmother had died but he kept remembering his father's advice, 'Take care with them beti, boy', and understood that his father's advice had come from experience.

Father Sebastian had a distinct sense of loss. The soul of Cecile Monagas had slipped through his consecrated fingers; young and nervous like a bride on her first night.

He imagined a young bird, fluttering, trapped in a house: the fear of the bird and the fear it engendered in the witness and perpetrator of its entrapment and in him, the person trying to free it, struggling with its rescuer. He was pained by the reverberations of its struggle and its attempt to find an open window.

In the last days it lay still as the body gave up living and the skin seemed to fade over the bones, transparent, so that the soul could slip through. When he anointed her body he did it in the belief that it had been a tabernacle.

The celibate had wooed her soul for Christ. Each morning she brought him her fear.

She had formulated her sin. She could not remember whether she had consummated her marriage.

'Father I can't remember. I am denying my husband his right.'

'My child look at your daughter.'

'But Father I pray to Our Lady of the Immaculate Conception.'

He attempted to remind her of the evidence of her life: her daughter who had lived; the baptisms she had administered; the memory of the nine little angels assumed into heaven. He reminded her of the taffeta-quilted, white satin coffins under the earth in Paradise Cemetery.

But each morning the amnesia returned as she woke with her heart fluttering like the wings of the trapped bird: waking with Carlos near to her before he left to descend to the orchid house for the morning inspection, but not being able to remember. There was a lid over her dreams, memories, as vast as the lid over the gulf; a grey shadow, the Holy Spirit brooding over the waters at the beginning of creation, overshadowing her.

Father Sebastian absolved her so that she could make a new start, each day a new start to try and remember. Then Carlos had died.

Father Sebastian dozed off in his underpants and vest under the whirring fan as he reminded himself that he must tell the sexton to toll the bells.

The mourners began to arrive at the house standing about the yard in little groups; the relatives and the white friends. In the church the women of the Legion of Mary had begun the fifteen mysteries of the rosary.

The grave-diggers endured their vigil with tots of rum, leaning on their forks and spades sunk into the wet earth after they had tidied away the rotting planks of Carlos's coffin and overcome their astonishment at the remnants of the nine white satin coffins.

Alicia could not stay inside her room, battened down in the servants' quarters off the courtyard, outside the kitchen. There was no air. The trees did not stir and there was not a sound of a bird. There was only the monotony of the town and a little nearer the drip of the pipe in the orchid house. She dragged her stool under the arch which opened on to the path to the orchid house and the sunken garden. She liked to sit there because she could see the sea from there.

'So Madam gone,' she said to herself with her one hundred years. She stared at the sea and the swoop of the circling corbeaux over the gulf.

The wreaths began to arrive at the house and at the church piled up in the doorways, at the back of cars and on top of the hearse standing in the yard at the front of the blue-stone house; beginning to suffocate the atmosphere with the perfume of their dying blooms.

The women in the flower shops brushed up the wilting sweet-lime leaves and the dust of the asparagus fern.

Father Sebastian had woken and showered and put on a clean white cassock. He sat in his rattan rocker on the verandah of the presbytery behind the ledge with the pots of eucharist lilies reciting the Magnificat: 'My soul doth magnify the Lord'.

The Indian music, the transistors and the stereo taxis kept up their incessant screech and throb.

These last preparations for the obsequies of Cecile Monagas de los Macajuelos did not penetrate the sunless, shuttered and sweating room at the back of Teresa's Hairdressing Salon. Gaston had forgotten about his car parked in the gutter and that he was to be a pall-bearer. It was creating a traffic jam in the High Street and no one had any idea whose it was, so careful had he been about his incognito. Two policemen kept walking around it, writing down the registration number and the number of the licence and tax disc into little black books and then walking away again. Taxi drivers shouted and gesticulated at it and pedestrians waiting for a taxi leant up on it allowing Coca-Cola and curry juice from *barras* to drip on to it. None of this entered the emptied brain of Gaston. His activity had created a state of amnesia.

Marie-Claire had arrived back at the house in the same sweating afternoon to receive her sister's body from Samaroo's. She had powdered her nose and tidied her grey hair into a bun at the nape of her neck and wore a lilac dress. She had on a white hat with a tulle veil to blur her tears. She stood on the terrace with a cloud of blue plumbago and white Queen Anne's lace in front of her. She stared out over the gulf towards the mountains; the foothills of the Andes rising to the heights of Venezuela over the archipelago of linking islands, beyond the island of Patos.

'Aunty what you staring at?' Mariana called from the window upstairs. 'Mr Samaroo should be here any minute.'

'Just thinking dear.' She kept on staring, remembering. She remembered her mother and grandmother whose ancestor rode on his horse beside Bolivar.

The leaden lid of the vault would once again open to receive one of her own. She stared at the gulf.

The gulf stared back at her. This was the gulf into which the ships with the slaves of Lopinot and Roume St Laurent had sailed. This was the gulf into which had sunk the burning galleons of Apodoca; the English, French and Spanish ships of plunder. This was the gulf into which had flowed the blood of suicidal Amerindians claiming themselves in death rather than capture. Into this gulf had flowed the disinfectant from off the bodies of indentured Indians whose children and women ate clay in the quarantine camps on the island of Nelson. It was from the waters of this gulf that the baptisms were administered to innocent people. And it was along the shores of this gulf that a young black girl of fourteen had strolled, smoking a cigar, and had later been taken to an upper room in the port and tortured with the chains of the Inquisition.

The gulf stared back, inscrutable and metallic. Marie-Claire arranged a strand of stray grey hair behind her ear and into the folds of her bun. She thought about her own death.

Mr Samaroo delivered the coffin, lifting it carefully, with the help of attendants, into the drawing-room where the murmur of the rosary continued like the tide. Five mysteries of the rosary were recited while the relatives and white friends crushed through the front doors into the hallway, overflowing on to the terraces, until the house was once again a house for a funeral. Women fanned themselves and the men mopped their brows, sweating in their stuffed suits. Eau-de-Cologne and Chanel No. 5 dripped in the perspiration.

'Where is that son of mine?' Mariana came and knelt near to Marie-Claire who was praying into the open coffin.

'Leave it in God's hands, my dear.' Marie-Claire continued with the rosary fingering the crystal beads.

'I wish I could say that he was in God's hands now, instead of you know whose arms.' Mariana stifled her anger out of respect for her mother and because she did not want to cause an embarrassment.

The five mysteries faded into the ejaculations for the dead. The pall-bearers came to lift the coffin. Mr Samaroo, with generations of etiquette and respect, substituted for Gaston.

The doors of the hearse were shut and the last stages of Cecile Monagas de los Macajuelos' funeral procession began to wind its way slowly down from the top of Mount Mora; from the top of the hill with the fir trees in the garden of the blue-stone house overlooking the gulf. It descended, one car behind the other, behind the hearse: brakes creaking, bumpers almost scratching the chrome of the other; each car packed with family, weighted down and suffocating under wreaths stacked behind the back seats and on the bonnets. The procession descended into the jangling, tumble-down town: sweating, throbbing and locked in an inextricable traffic jam, because unknown to them all, family and friends, Gaston's car was holding up the traffic in the High Street, parked in front of Teresa's Hairdressing Salon.

Waiting in the church, the people of the town congregated: the black people who had known Miss Monagas; the women of the Legion of Mary both the Junior and Senior Praesidiums; representatives from the Catholic Youth Organisation; the first communion classes and the confirmation classes; the Catholic wing of the Girl Guides and Boy Scouts; nurses from the Red Cross who had laboured over the body of Carlos Monagas; members of the Horticultural Society who had gone to the blue-stone house for orchid exhibitions; the Society of the Sacred Heart; children of Our Lady of Fatima and Our Lady of Lourdes packed the aisles and the porticoes of the side-doors. Black people who usually congregated on the bandstand opposite the Town Hall and Indians who sat on the railings around the statue of Mahatma Gandhi came too, pulled by this throng which had taken centuries to collect. Members of the Protestant community, business associates and the Freemasons took their places.

As four o'clock approached the Mother Superior of the convent of Cluny proceeded across the promenade with her community of nuns following, heads bowed beneath their fluttering linen veils.

Father Sebastian proceeded down the aisle in his capacious black satin cope, billowing out behind him, preceded by acolytes carrying holy water buckets, thuribles with burning coals for incense and candles. They took up their positions at the entrance of the church to receive the body of Cecile Monagas de los Macajuelos.

Father Sebastian had remembered the bells and he had ordered the sexton to begin tolling them at five minutes to four o'clock.

The clergy from the neighbouring parishes and the abbot of the monastery in the mountains filled the sanctuary. The church was dense with prayer and talcum powder.

The ancestral funeral procession took years to battle through the traffic of the centuries and the streets. The people of the town waited for the cortege and the day to progress to the church and thence to Paradise Cemetery.

The procession was stuck in Cipero Street. The High Street was jammed. The orange-sellers, the peanut and channa-vendors at the library corner did a good trade with passengers hanging out of stationary taxis.

Gaston, the last descendant of the Monagas de los Macajuelos, who in these last days were famed for their still gargantuan stature, the mysterious circulation of their blood and the complexity of their digestive systems, had brought the town to a standstill. The projectors in the Radio City, the Rivoli, the Gaiety and the Globe flickered and went out over the matinee performances because no one could get to see them; Maureen O'Hara dying in the arms of Randolph Scott; the massacre of the North American Indians and the crimes of Chicago gangsters.

The people of the town of San Andres stood on the pavements and looked on at what was taking a long time to pass away. The Bible preachers began their sermons of repentance between hallelujahs and the Baptist women lit their candles and rang their bell calling the people together. People were reminded to look at what was passing away and what was taking its place.

The funeral cortege sat in their misted up Mitsubishis, Toyotas,

113

Mazdas, long American and chunky British limousines, refrigerated by air-conditioning.

At five minutes to four o'clock Father Sebastian sent an acolyte to give the sexton the signal to start with the tolling of the bells.

At each successive boom, the tolling of the funeral bells eventually penetrated the sunless and shuttered room at the back of Teresa's Hairdressing Salon. They eventually bored their way through the amnesiacal barrier into Gaston's memory. He suddenly remembered as he lay there, sweating, that this was the day that his grandmother had died and he was a pall-bearer.

He leapt out of bed and picked up his pants from off the floor. 'Girl, ah go see yuh,' he said as he dashed out into the street pulling up his pants and buttoning his crotch.

The congested town heaved forward with the moving of Gaston's car. It was already growing dark when the funeral procession eventually arrived at the church. Father Sebastian had buried the other dead. The Saint John Ambulance Brigade had attended to the fainting congregation.

The last obsequies were rushed so that Cecile could be buried before nightfall as the law stipulated.

The last shovel of earth was packed down on to the grave. Gaston's father patted him on the shoulder and said, 'Too much beti, boy.'

Alicia, helped along with her one hundred years by Madoo, shook her head as she left the cemetery, 'So madam gone, eh Madoo, madam gone.'